MY STORY

we lose ourselves in the beings we love,
we find ourselves too

STORY my

ERIN KANOA

ARTEMYS PRESS

Books may be purchased in quantity and/or special sales by contacting
the publisher, Artemys Press, Bellingham, WA 98225
email at: info@erinkanoa.com

Photography by Erin Kanoa

Layout, Cover and Design by Artemys Press
Cataloging-in-publication data

First Artemys Press edition 2016
ISBN: 978-0-9973463-8-1

Published by Artemys Press

For more information, please contact Erin Kanoa at Artemys Press
10 9 8 7 6 5 4 3 2 1

to the love that connects
dog and human

We communicate through singing tones, images and energy, eye contact and feeling, living the great story that has run in us and through us for generation after generation. We understand humans the same way, through their tones, their energy, scents and movements. We feel the vibration that emanates from all living things in this world, and are driven by instinct and prowess, loyalty to the pack, and now, by honoring the Code between human and dog.

You have to understand. For millions of years, our canine tribe has been watching you, observing you from both afar and up close. Sure, at first to see if you would taste good, and indeed sometimes you did.

In time, you made tools and fire; and those things made it much more difficult to hunt you. But we watched, and kept observing as our hunting grounds covered the same areas and our lives became intertwined. We noticed you were watching us also, for soon you hunted as we did - as one. We taught you the power of the pack, *of thinking of each other, of thinking of your young as a group.*

But as your numbers grew, we became more curious; we would rest near your fires, we would watch you eat and you would toss us scraps of food. And, yes, on a few occasions, you would come across one of us injured or dying. Sometimes you would kill us right there for our skin, our flesh, other times you would leave us. As we saw you move across the land, we would linger, not to harm you or hunt you, but to watch you, to feel your intention as fellow hunters.

It was during a hunt on the plains, that an early blizzard came on with such ferocity that a lone human hunter was lost in the white. Unable to see or keep moving, he hunkered down to survive. At the same time, a Dire wolf mother with two cubs had become separated from her pack. She was slower and in tow of the young pups from a late fall birth. The hunter and this wolf came face to face. He was too tired and frozen to fight, and she was too tired and frozen to try and kill him. Her pups were her greatest concern now. Both knew they could die alone or survive together, so they huddled together through the night. The snow piled deep around them, but their combined heat and the pelts the hunter carried kept them alive. The night of survival had forged a gentle peace.

As dawn broke, surrounded by a deep blanket of snow, the wolf was unable to find the scent of her pack. The man, feeling the gratitude of being alive, saw her plight and chose not to try and kill her but instead slowly make his way back to his group, encouraging her and the dear pups to follow. But the snow was too deep, and the little ones were unable to keep pace, so the man slowed, giving them bits of food as encouragement. The wolf mother was grateful for the compassion shown.

By late morning, they made it to the small camp, tucked in a mix of tree branches and deer hides. A woman and two children were gathering wood. A fire was going. The woman was overjoyed to see her mate back alive, after his absence through the night. But upon seeing the wolf approaching, she shrieked in fear. His hands went up, conveying she should be calm, and then she saw the pups. The woman's eyes opened wider as the wolf sat, just beyond the edge of the clearing; the little ones leaning into her long front legs.

The man explained what had happened and how he was able to survive the night. The woman hugged him close, while the children hugged both their legs. She then looked to the mama wolf and invited them to all come closer. It was connection between two mothers, who loved their young more than anything. That evening, the wolf and her pups were fed by humans, not her pack. That evening the lives of wolf and human were changed forever.

Today was the day she would make it beyond the fence. Just past dawn, under the wide open blue skies of Walla Walla, Washington, a young Border Collie saw her path to freedom. The days of being left alone to hearing sounds that were not there, random harassment by passing flies, and pacing a well-worn track around the yard were coming to an end. She dug furiously, her paws deftly creating an ever-widening gap beneath the wire. Dirt flew in all directions, coating her fur by the second; her tongue hung inches out of her mouth; her breathing became labored. But none of these discomforts would be stopping her. It had been over a year in the making and her decision had not come lightly, for she loved humans, but these humans were not following the Code. And so today was the day Mama chose to escape. Today was the day my story would begin.

As Mama went on to share the details of digging a hole deep and wide enough to crawl under without getting stuck, I found my attention wandering to the fly crawling on the living room window. Mama paused for a moment, to catch my eye. She had a very deliberate way about her, very focused, and she expected the same of us. But our attention was still being honed, and our exuberance spilled into everything we did, including sitting still long enough to listen to this story! We were puppies, after all.

To keep myself occupied, while keeping still, I studied Mama's face as she spoke. She had a symmetrical pattern of bright black and white soft fur. The tip of her nose was shiny, wet black. The fur that led from her nose was also bright white, the opposite color of my all-black muzzle. The band of white continued up her forehead and ended between her ears. A black mask of fur started at the tip's of her ears and draped down over her head, wrapping around the white muzzle, and down her shoulders. Her deep, tawny brown eyes glistened against the black, with a steady, yet loving gaze. She was beautiful. She was perfect. She was Mama.

As I drifted back into the story, she had made it under the fence and was not far from the house, when she noticed a big dog named Jasper was following her. Jasper was a large, loving, black Lab stud, with the kindest of souls. But Jasper had one thing on his mind: making more Jaspers. So when Mama, a young, pure Border Collie in heat, came cruising by (and by cruising by, she meant passing by at a distance of a half-mile), he felt compelled to see if she was interested in some short-term companionship.

Well, she wasn't. She was a filthy mess and feeling a little crazy running from the sounds that were not there. Not to mention, he was a Lab! No, no, no, no, no. When the time was right, she was supposed to be with another Border Collie! But he persisted, and after a mile or so of nonstop sweet talk, and a large amount of pheromones exchanged, she could no longer resist. And so, quite by accident, her escape set into motion the circumstances for all of us puppies to come into the world.

Under a mid-afternoon sky, they said their good-byes. Jasper headed toward home and Mama kept on her way, trotting across field after golden field. The trotting had softened her loneliness, as she focused on the new shapes and smells she came across. But her dry tongue reminded her she had not drank all day and was now far away from anything that looked or even smelled familiar.

She sniffed the air for any scent that would lead her to water. Some dark green bushes were lined up along the far edge of the field she was crossing. The wind was not coming from that direction, but green bushes meant water, so she headed toward them. What she found was a small ditch of putrid water, so she kept following the line of bushes a ways, until it led to a nearby creek. Although it was very small, the water was flowing and clear, and she drank eagerly.

After her long drink, she began to relax, but knew night was coming. She chose a grove of large trees on a soft rise above the fields. Once at the top, she could still hear the small creek gurgling below and also look out in all directions. It would be the perfect place to spend the night.

Her day-long journey had not led her near any humans, which was okay, she told us. The memory of the yard, the lack of love and attention, was still very fresh in her mind. She wanted to calm herself, let the unsettling energy of living with those humans fade away. She wanted to be composed, and proud when finding her new home. Mama was very collected that way.

As the evening light grew, she looked out across the land. The swallows were catching the last few bugs of the day, the crickets had started to chirp, and a soft, warm breeze came up, bringing all kinds of smells past her nose. The stars began to appear one by one, stirring a distant, familiar feeling of comfort. She had found shelter for the night, and a relaxed tiredness settled softly on her. Though she went to sleep hungry, the feeling was overshadowed by a fullness of calm, of being out in the open, under the stars, sung to by crickets.

She dreamt that night of digging and running in the golden fields, of hearing things that were not there, of the fence, of drinking from the tiny creek. She woke several times, thinking she was back in the yard. Finally, she surrendered to her exhaustion and curled tightly against the base of a tree, where she fell into a deep sleep.

The next morning, it was hunger that woke her up. That, and a mildly stiff rear leg from lying on the hard ground. But she set aside those concerns as she stretched in the glory of the sunrise. She described for us the awe of watching the colors of the sky change. Blues went to light yellows and pinks. Soon an orange glow crawled up the horizon. Listening to her, a deep joy welled up, as if we had been right next to her. We saw through her eyes and were amazed.

She described the birds chirping, the frogs singing, the sound of a slight breeze shifting the leaves of the branches above. How she felt connected to the subtle energies of all the living things around her, including the very trees she slept under.

Within her awe of the moment, she realized she had to find breakfast. Never having to catch her own food before, she wasn't sure what she would find, but the scent of mice was strong in the fields, and so that's where she decided to start. They were small and fast, but many in number. And so she began to master the art of mouse catching. Her first few attempts were horrible misses, she admitted, and was glad no one was around to witness them, for she was very proud of her pure lineage and the great agility that ran in her family. But she sensed that with practice, it would get easier, as an inner stirring was guiding her moves. By mid-morning she had caught three!

We were all in awe of how she could catch something so small and fast. We had only seen a mouse near the garbage, and it was quite elusive. Mama went on to explain that mouse catching was a job that required good scenting ability, immense patience, and what she liked to call the 'mouse pounce,' an artful jumping move she promised to show us the next day outside.

Over the first several mornings, as she enjoyed catching mice, a natural routine emerged, allowing her to relax in a way she had not known before. She felt the sounds that were not there begin to subside, and began hearing the world around her as it was.

Over the passing days, she developed a knack for catching mice, but in doing so she created a problem for herself. The number of mice around the trees had dwindled, and she had to go further and further away to catch them. On the way back from one of her hunting passes, she came across the scat of a coyote. She explained that a coyote was a lot like us, but it would hunt mice and sheep and cats, and even dogs, when hungry enough. Her Mama had taught her that neither they, nor their words were to be trusted, ever, as coyotes followed a different Code. Finding the scat sent an uneasy chill through her. Where there was one, there were usually more, and she was very much alone and in their territory. That evening she did not sleep much at all.

The following morning, still feeling a bit unsettled, she decided to stay closer to the trees. A few rabbits were out in the field close by, and she set her sights on catching one of them. That, she said, took a whole different strategy. She

had to be still and wait. And wait, and wait, and wait some
more. But once she was within a few body lengths of a
rabbit, she could chase it down no problem, and the meal
would fill her for days. It was on one of her patient waits
for a rabbit, someone found her. A large, long, thick dirt-
colored creature came weaving across the ground, nearly
hidden in the grass until it was about a body length away
from her. She froze. The creature had a repetitive pattern
along its back, and a strange, long, shiny, light colored
lumpy bump on its tail, and a head with cold, golden eyes.
Its thin, split-tipped tongue flickered in and out rapidly. She
had never seen anything like it. It had very little scent. Even
her Highland memories had not prepared her for such an
creature.

As it sniffed the air, it smoothly wove away from her
through the grass, then it was gone. Her senses strongly told
her avoid, avoid, avoid, threat, threat! But how could she
avoid it, if she couldn't see it, let alone smell it?

Mama had now woken to many sunrises and relaxed to many sunsets. But one evening, while gazing at the stars, she felt a deep stirring in her lower belly. Amidst the random hunger pains from the day's hunt not going in her favor, she sensed a new energy growing inside her. Our presence was taking shape; she was not alone anymore. Small energy pulses were aligning, as if forming a constellation for each of us. She had pups on the way and felt each of us start to dance inside her. "Little Stars," she called us, meaning we were all a part of the universe. Generation after generation of Border Collies had spent nights, just like this one, looking up at the stars, while stars grew inside of them.

Over the next half moon cycle, she managed to navigate around the local rattlesnake and the curious coyote. In the evenings, she mulled over the question of what was best. She had to think about more than herself now. Already she was more hungry, gaining weight around her middle, and her mouse pounce was losing its bounce. But could she find another family to take her in? Would they take her in? She could see no houses from her spot in the trees, and how long would it take her to get to one? As far as she knew, no other humans were around for her to go to. She told us then how bonding with your human was an amazing feeling. Her mama had had such a bond, and her mama before her. It was, as she said, "the way." And so now, without a human, she was in very unfamiliar territory.

She could go it alone, but she had no consistent food or a fully safe place to rest, and she would be needing more and more food for the next few months. Each time she left the trees to catch mice, she knew she was being watched by one or more coyotes. The next morning, after much patient work, she caught another rabbit and devoured it, but she would not be able to hunt like that after the next moon. She began feeling a pressure she had not experienced, a pressure to feel safe. Her sense of adventure was diminishing. She instead wanted to protect the life inside of her.

The trees gave her shelter from the sun during the day and from the dew at night. They were old, and had stood strong through many seasons; their strength gave her a sense of security and peace. She was tempted to stay among them, but the trees could not fully protect her from the snake or the coyote, nor could they feed her and her pups. After deep consideration, she reluctantly decided to go back to the yard.

We were stunned. Mama knew what we were about to ask, and this time, she let us.

"Why did you go back?"

She began to share the urge to keep us safe and alive. She explained her humans had not harmed her. They'd fed her and given her a home, but she had not felt love, the fulfillment of the bond she knew should be strong. This was sounding familiar to me.

"We are back where you escaped from, aren't we?" I asked her.

"Yes," Mama replied.

There it was, the cold reality laid at our paws. We were not in a good home. We were not in a home Mama felt good about at all! On some level, we knew already.

Mama was silent. She had our full attention now. I wasn't sure what she was feeling. It was many feelings all at once. But then I sensed her clarity. Mama's eyes sharpened.

"Little ones, I have shared this story with you because I want us all to escape together."

Escape?! We were going to escape also? Just like Mama? No wonder she gave us the details on digging a hole under a fence. She was planning our escape!

After learning of Mama's plan, we could not be contained. We were interested, yet agitated, and outside was the place to go when we felt pent up. So out the dog door we went, to take in some fresh air and light. The grass felt warm on our paws as we squatted to pee and run around a bit. Mama let us take a moment as we gathered in a loose formation around her, then continued the story of her return to the house.

The woman had opened the door, and the familiar, stale house smell wafted out; the talking screen was on in the empty living room. She greeted Mama wholeheartedly and began to cry. Getting a hug was nice, and Mama was happy the man was not there. As Mama's food bowl was filled until it spilled out onto the floor, she noticed the slowness of the woman's movements and the bitter smell on her breath. While Mama dug into her food, the woman's tears welled up again.

Mama said she felt the woman's sadness and apology in the tone of her voice, and it comforted her. A kind moment was shared between them, a concern for Mama's well-being; maybe things could change. Maybe her leaving had caused the woman to see what she had done?

So Mama crawled into her old, stinky bed and fell fast asleep to the drone of the talking screen. In the quiet of the night, she awoke briefly and missed the stars, the sounds of the chirping crickets, and the gentle-strong trees. But then she thought of us, growing inside her, that her belly was full, that we were safe from the snake and the coyote, and that settled her heart.

Mama was roused in the morning by the sounds of the woman getting breakfast going. As the woman sipped her coffee, she looked over at Mama with her brow furrowed, conveying astonishment. She muttered to herself as she got dressed, something about Mama needing to look a little better.

It must have been one of the days the woman stayed home, because she was not rushing off as usual. After breakfast, they were in the car with the windows down. They arrived at the groomer. It was during the bath he noted Mama's belly. The two humans had a discussion, and the woman realized Mama was carrying puppies.

What Mama didn't know, was the man and woman had plans to breed her with another Border Collie, but had waited through her first estrus, hoping to find a suitable sire. Once they realized an unknown siring had happened, their disappointment became obvious. The man showed his contempt by scoffing at Mama whenever she came near him. The woman was a little softer in her disdain, but she drank the tainted liquid so often Mama said you could never be sure of her. She did, however, get Mama special food and made a place for her in the bedroom. The man wasn't very happy about it and kept saying unkind words towards Mama.

But Mama held herself proud in the presence of such statements. She was a dog. The chosen companion of the human race. She also came from a long line of outstanding Border Collies on both sides. She was worthy of much more than the setting she now found herself in.

Almost a whole moon cycle had passed, and Mama felt us begin to move in her belly with the energy of wanting to be born. Lucky for Mama, the woman had a friend who knew about whelping puppies. She came over that night and helped Mama give birth to us all. But something wasn't right when the last one of us came out, and Mama was stressed. The birth of the last pup tore Mama in such a way that now she was bleeding.

The friend noticed, and within moments a kind man arrived. He carried a large cloth bag, and saw Mama's distress, and began soothing her by petting her head and sharing kind words with her. He had a gentle heart with a soul to match. He reminded Mama of Jasper, and this helped put her at ease. When she saw a very sharp object being placed near her thigh, she looked into the man's heart and saw his intentions were good. The neighbor was also talking sweetly to her, telling her it was okay, she would be okay. So Mama relaxed. She described that at first it hurt, but not long after, all her pain lessened. She was too tired to question things, but less pain allowed her to take full breaths again. The kind man then attended to her bleeding, making some small stitches to close her up. But as he finished, he said words that made the neighbor sad and caused the woman to frown.

As she looked at Mama's pups, the woman became angry, and unkind words were being directed at Mama.

Mama, though exhausted and foggy, felt the spiteful energy of the woman, and shielded us with her body. She looked to the kind man and then to the neighbor, asking with her eyes to please take us all. They just looked back at her lovingly. The kind man softly stroked her side, and said loving words towards her and her pups. She wanted to go with him, but he carefully gathered his things. All she could do was watch the door close behind him.

The neighbor stayed close for the next little while, as Mama licked us. Mama described the neighbor as someone who truly loved dogs, who loved us for who we were. This was how it should be, she reminded us.

We agreed. We knew 'Jessica' as she was called, was the nice lady who would come over from time to time, and we all wished we could live with her.

My heart went out to Mama. Why had she thought that coming back would change anything? Yet after hearing about the process, I was glad we hadn't been born out in the dirt with a coyote waiting to eat us.

The neighbor stayed and petted Mama softly, she was

sad to see her go also. Mama then curled up around us, very much looking forward to seeing Jessica the next morning.

Although she was exhausted, Mama couldn't fully relax, having felt the spiteful energy of the woman. Her mind raced, wondering how this would affect us. In Mama's eyes, we all were her Little Stars, but she understood we were not pure in the eyes of humans. To the man and woman, we were less than desirable. Mama was not happy knowing her babies would be seen as anything other than perfect. She realized things were not going to change in this place. That's when she'd started planning for the right moment to get us all away.

Our birth night didn't end in peaceful sleep for Mama. A short while after we were born, she said, we were nursing and very content. Mama had dozed off herself, only to wake to my twin sister, off the teat. She was the fragile one, the last one born, and a bit smaller than I was. Mama nudged her with her muzzle, but she just didn't want the teat. Mama pulled her close to us to keep her warm, but she was very still, and much cooler than us.

The woman came back in to check on Mama and noticed the little one seemed to be struggling. The woman was less grumpy, Mama said, and quietly sat and watched, while petting Mama's head, saying very soft, kind words.

Mama nudged the little pup, and continued to lick her forcefully, but the little one remained still, growing colder, and soon stopped breathing.

A somber Mama laid her head down next to the cold pup. The woman had dozed a bit in her chair, and now came over and saw the little one's frail body, separated from the rest of us. She bent down to touch her, knew it was dead, and began to cry. She then picked her up and held her to her chest. Mama was surprised when the woman let out a quiet wail.

She reached over, gently touched Mama on the head, and kissed her. Mama smelled an unfamiliar scent on the woman; it was grief. She felt the heat and anguish in it. When Mama looked up into the woman's eyes, she saw loss and sadness and the isolation from bearing great pain. The woman's heart had opened in seeing this loss in another, even a dog. It was the first moment of true compassion Mama had felt from the woman, who now looked deeply into Mama's eyes. The woman shared her memory vision; she too had lost a baby. She sat on the blanket with Mama and broke down sobbing.

Mama's story was a lot for us take in, and I was feeling a unique angst in the moment. I was the only one who didn't look like Mama? I had a twin sister? Life could end? And I looked more like my daddy, Jasper, but not quite? I instantly felt out of place, as all my siblings had longer, fluffy, multicolored fur. I now felt strangely separate from Mama; I couldn't look her in the eye.

As my siblings ran out their own energies, I finally looked over at Mama, stunned. She understood. Where did I fit in? Until today, it hadn't occurred to me that I was different from my brothers or sisters, or that I was undesirable in the eyes of humans. She nuzzled me and rolled me over in play. I felt the blending of her love and her sadness towards me.

In that moment, I was pulled deeply into Mama's eyes. The grass I was sitting on, the sounds of my siblings frolicking, the temperature of the air, the bird flying overhead, all faded away. Her eyes grew around me until I was in another realm.

It was cold, my fur tingled, then brightness glowed around me as wide open vistas of vivid green rolling hills spread out in all directions. A blue expanse of sky floated above me. Out past the green below, I could see a large, shimmering distant pulsing, shifting blue. It was water, large water with specks of shifting white. Sparse, black, rock outcroppings dotted the landscape, casting gray shadows all around. The scent was musty and salty, damp and pungent.

Round, soft, white forms milled in the distance, nibbling the grass and chewing it calmly. I listened to their murmuring sounds to each other. One of them walked over to me. It had floppy ears and was covered in curly, woolen hair. Its eyes were kind and gentle.

I looked for Mama, but she was not around. A jolt ran through my body. "Where's Mama?" Then I saw her eyes again, her face, and I was back on the warm grass in the yard. My brother was now playing with sis, pushing on me with his back leg.

Mama looked deeply into my eyes and warmth filled my heart. "This is who you are, little one," she conveyed silently. "This is who we are."

I had no idea what had just happened, but a feeling of belonging filled my senses. While Mama gave her attention to the others, I began to absorb what I had seen. It was Mama's world I had been in, right? But somehow I'd been there. And now I felt that world in me. It felt more real to me than anything I knew, so big and fresh and alive, such a contrast to the life around me.

That night, and many nights after, I went to sleep and returned to Mama's inner world; faint, random, mental images grew vivid. I began to know her life and to see into the lives beyond her; into her mama's life, and her mama's mama's life and beyond.

Sometimes we were in a new place with new animals: a dank forest with bright sunlight streaming in through the branches above; or a moonlit meadow during wintertime, with the frost glistening, a chill on our breath. A misty rain would fall and we would sit, watching over the flock. The colors of the seasons turned from yellow to green to blue. Smells and scents, aligned with their sources, encouraging my senses to grow and learn. The movements and faces of the humans in the meadow with the sheep gained meaning. In turn, they would signal us, we would respond. They would watch our bodies, we heard the meaning of their tones, and glean the intent. We moved through the flocks of sheep and onto the tall rocks to survey from above. The wind blew our fur, and I grew to love the wind, for it brought messages in the dreamtime. I learned its meanings: friendly human, curious wolf, hungry mouse, or hunting cat.

Over the next few weeks, I spent more time in the dreamtime. We were all lighter of heart, knowing we would be getting away with Mama soon. We were eating well, growing fast, and learning so much! Even the grumpy man had a few chuckles at our frolicking and general goofiness.

But then people we had never seen started coming over. They would pick up my brother and Mindy and Cindy (the woman had named the twins to keep them straight). No one looked at me or called me over, so I tried to stay close to Mama, but she was panting and pacing about these new people touching her pups.

"Don't touch them, I don't know you!" her actions said.

She pawed someone's legs, urging him to let go of Mindy.

The human said some words to her that showed he did

not understand what she wanted.

Mama dared not bite a human, so she flattened her ears and let out a soft growl.

"Anna! No!" the woman said sternly.

Mama backed away but did not take her eyes off Mindy until the man set her down. Mindy then ran to Mama, and we all stayed close. My heart was racing. Mama's thoughts spread to us all; we needed to escape sooner than even she had thought.

Mama could not have known the timeliness of telling her story, and of getting us ready to escape, for not a half moon cycle after the people came, Mindy was taken. And the day after that, Cindy was too.

The day Mindy was taken, Mama spent until evening looking for her; under the bed, behind the couch, all over the yard. She did this, even after seeing her go out the door with a plump, strong-scented woman. The next day, as Cindy was being taken, Mama let out a cry. A howl that sent shivers into my heart. The pain Mama felt permeated my soul, and I began to shake. I didn't know what was her pain and what was mine.

She continued her cry as she ran out to the yard, watching through the fence as the car drove away with Cindy. We helplessly followed her, feeling the loss of our sisters begin to settle in. Our pack was broken. We sat together by the fence until sundown, uninterested in food when the woman set out our dinner.

From then on, Mama kept us away from the woman as much as she could. She wouldn't eat. And as much as brother and I tried to cheer her up, nothing worked. My heart felt lost with her sadness. As Mama laid on the ground; I would lay next to her head, licking her as she stared into the deep emptiness. Mindy and Cindy were gone. My brother and I had to work together, and help Mama to get out of here as soon as possible.

But Mama was in no condition. Her spark and light were dim. Jessica would come over at some point in the day, and pick me up, and ask me kind questions, with such love in her eyes. She was the only one who ever held me, so I would hold nothing back and promptly lick her face all over.

She would laugh heartily, showering me with kind words in all forms. I would lick and nuzzle her more, knowing how happy it made her. Mama enjoyed seeing me loved by someone so much, she would finally get up and join in. Eventually we would all end up on the floor, licking and getting petted, basically just having a great time.

After a few days of Jessica visiting, Mama started to act like herself again. She held her head higher and knew we still had a chance. So she started eating more and told us to do the same. We were getting out of here in the next few days.

It was clear that even with her strange ways, the woman loved Mama as best she could. But now that Mindy and Cindy were gone, any attention given to my brother or me was lessening. A few nights after Cindy was taken, they made brother and I sleep apart from Mama. I whined for Mama to come, but it didn't matter to the humans. No one came, not even Mama. In the morning, Mama rushed in, wagging and licking us enthusiastically.

"Oh, my dears, how are you? I heard your cries, but they wouldn't let me go to you!"

Each morning after, she looked more and more stressed. I told her we were okay, but we both knew I was lying. Mama reassured us that she loved us. We would get out of here once she got some strength back. So in the day we played and laughed with Jessica, and listened to stories about the Highlands, where Mama's family came from. She was doing her best to keep us busy.

One evening, as they put us in the back room, Mama felt strong enough to challenge that decision. She stood in front of the door and would not come away. The man moved towards her with anger, and her ears went back.

Mama was between us and him and did not move. He smacked her across the face.

Stunned, I felt brother's energy to rush and help, but Mama gave him the eye. With her head down, she solemnly left to the other part of the house. My heart ached to see her treated this way, and now so defeated and forced to slink away from us against her will. Why could we not sleep with Mama anymore? This made no sense to me. We had to get out of here!

The door was shut, the lights were out, and brother and I trembled in our basket. Never had we seen a human hit one of us, not to mention our Mama. I wanted to be with her so badly, to snuggle into her fur and fall asleep to her heartbeat. Brother and I did our best to comfort each other. It was so dark, and we were alone, this was not the way things were supposed to happen.

The more I thought about it, the more unsettled I felt. My heart started to race and I jumped out of the basket, sniffing the door, looking for a way out. Brother joined me, but there was no way out. We heard footsteps coming closer, and quickly jumped back in the basket, but the door did not open.

Thoughts swirled in my mind, how we could start digging first thing in the morning. With three of us, surely it would go much faster. It was hard to calm myself, but I focused my mind on getting beyond the fence the next morning and finding a new home with Mama and brother.

Later, I found myself in the dreamtime, and the feeling was more vivid than my last visits. Mama was right next to me. I wasn't seeing through her eyes, I was here with her as my self. The sky was a miraculous combination of blue and gray twilight hues. The ocean breeze was chilly; the salty air calmed me. The sheep were lying down around us, content. All was peaceful.

Within the scene I sensed a presence, and the hairs on my back bristled. A Mama-shaped glowing silhouette appeared on the rocky rise before us. She was quite a bit taller, and much wider, bigger in every proportion. Mama could have easily walked under this beasts belly, and never touch the belly fur. As she came closer, her colors were silver and gray all over. Her legs were strong and her body was stout. She was massive.

I started to shake, and tucked in close to Mama's legs.

"It's okay, honey, she's one of us."

One of us? How could we ever be that big? But I stayed silent with that thought.

"She is very young," the giant dog stated.

"I didn't know she could make it. I wasn't sure she was able to," Mama replied calmly.

Mama then whispered to me, "This is your great ancestor, Brianna, the Dire wolf who first lived with humans. She has been the guide to our family for generations, and she is willing to be yours."

Brianna stepped down from the prominence and sat in front of us. She sniffed the air from our direction.

"She is part of you, yes?" Brianna offered in her stately tone.

"She is my pup, yes. I would like you to know her scent, so you can find her, if need be." Mama asked with great reverence.

I felt tingly all over. My hairs had calmed down, but my insides were ready to burst. I was still in awe at the size of this creature. Her fur was so thick, her paws so wide.

When she sniffed close to me, her large head was as big as my body. She gazed down at me with strong, gentle, knowing eyes and spoke softly with such grace and power.

"Little one, I am the source of your lineage and your instincts, keeper of the Code and your truest wisdom, and knower of 'the way'."

A hand roughly grabbed me in the dark. It was the man. He scooped me and brother up, one under each arm, and held us tight against his jacket. It smelled of smoke, stale oil, and unwashed human odor. I didn't like that smell, and now it was all around me. Brother squirmed to get free for that reason alone. He was fluffier than me, and his fur would get even more dirty and stinky than mine. So unless he liked a smell, he tried not to get smelled up by anyone or anything. The man took us, wrapped tightly in his arms, through the food place and out the front door. Mama was nowhere to be seen.

The dawn light was coming into the sky. Down the porch steps we went: bump, bump, bump, bump, bump. He took fast strides to the car, the gravel grinding beneath his boots, our heads bobbing up and down. The air was cold on my nose. Scents of dry, cut grass, dew, and fresh possum wafted by. As we neared the car, the grip of his arm tightened around my middle, causing enough pain to stop me from squirming. I exhaled and went limp. He would not let me go. Brother was feeling the pain, the scent of his fear blending with mine.

The man yanked on the truck door handle and then threw us in. The landing was softish, and the surface was cold, stinky. A puff of dander, hair, and ashes flew into my nose. I had only seen the outsides of these beasts; I had never been in one. Yuck! From the outside, they looked hard, shiny, dusty and sleek, dented, maybe a little rusty, but not so stinky.

The door slammed behind us. He opened another door in front and plopped down harshly on the seat. Another stink plume wafted in the air. The man pulled a long strip of fabric from the door side, turned to his other side, and I heard a click. His face was harder than it had been in the past few days, and there was something determined and directed about his actions. I could smell a distinct scent on him, the pique odor of anger.

He looked back at us, halting my rambling thoughts.

Angry, loud words followed.

His brow was furrowed, never a good sign with a human. The muscles in his jaw rippled, never, ever a good sign, and his voice was short, hard and deep, the worst sign of all!

He lit the stinky smoking stick that would hang out of his mouth and the truck began to hum. I began to whine for Mama. The seat rumbled beneath me, and at first nothing was moving, but as brother put his paws on the rear window, and trees started going by. The truck was moving away from the house.

"What? Where's Mama?"

I started to tremble and a dribble of pee came out. Where was Mama? We needed to go back!

As we bumped down the driveway, brother demanded, "This is wrong. Take us back!"

The man shot back even harsher, angrier words. I started to shake.

Shapes were now passing by the windows even faster. We had no fresh air, no outside smells, just a stale foulness with his breath mixed in with it. I was getting dizzy; my eyes had never moved so fast. I felt a little sick. I looked at brother and he looked back at me. I started to tremble, and brother sat next to me. His soft nuzzle told me, "I don't know what's going on, but at least we are together, and I am just as scared as you are."

"Where's Mama?" I said quietly to myself.

The shapes kept going by: wires, lights, cars, branches, sky, more wires, and tall poles, and more and more and more. I couldn't keep up, so I stopped looking out the window, and stayed focused on brother.

The sound of my pounding heart rushed through my ears. In one long, breathless moment, the filthy truck we were trapped in slowed down. The blurred colors of green, yellow and brown that had been flying by the dusty windows came into focus. They were stalks of grass, tall grass, that spread out as far as the eye could see.

As the truck pulled over to the side of the road, the crunching sound of gravel grew louder, until it growled to a stop. A cloud of dust boiled up, flew past the windows and drifted away. I looked out the window; where were we? Unexpected silence filled the space. The rush of blood in my ears lessened.

Brother turned his face from the window and our eyes connected with a glazed look. Fear, dread, sadness, and disbelief flowed between us. The heavy emotions, so thick and incomprehensible, left me immobilized and breathless. A soft whimper yearned to escape my muzzle. I started to let it out, but brother's eyes held mine. His black pupils grew large until only a thin, hazel edge remained.

"Stay silent," his eyes said. "Don't make a sound, sis."

His energy was strong and protective, so I listened. It brought me back to the present. We were in a grungy car, miles away from Mama.

The man turned around, his intentions still unkind. His eyes were hard and cold, angry and exhausted. In the low dawn light, the twisted lines on his face appeared deeper. The smoke from his ever-lit smoke maker filled the car with blue haze, casting a gray film over his features. But now a small hesitation, a gap, a pause, a silence filled the space we all shared. I sought his eyes directly. My fear submerged under a torrent of courage that flowed from my ancestors.

"Hear me now, you will listen to me."

I willed my thoughts to become his thoughts. My eyes stayed on his, my tail wagging beseechingly.

"Please take us back to Mama, please."

He heard me, inside his hardened soul, I knew it. The message had registered, but he shook it off and unbuckled his lap belt, then pushed the door open. A rush of cool, fresh air burst in around us. With a grunt, he lurched out of the car.

Once outside, he looked at us through the window, eyes cold, face hard. Our fear-filled eyes returned his gaze until the rear door swung open and a second rush of dew-damp air filled the cab.

"Well, thank goodness for that," I thought to myself, as the pungent, grassy aroma reached my nose. The stench of the car we had endured for the last half hour quickly dissipated. A faint scent of distant field mouse almost distracted me, but the cool rush of fresh air returned my senses to the moment.

The man yelled at us sternly. "Out!"

We trembled uncontrollably at that point, tails tucked hard against our pink bellies. Our toenails dug into the stained fabric of the filthy seat. As much as we had longed to be free during the ride, we now clung to the disgusting cushion for safety.

"Out!" he yelled a second time.

I felt a drop of pee ache for release.

Brother's eyes and mine were riveted on the man towering over us. We harnessed every ounce of mental persuasion, directing it with all our might, but the man would have none of it. He roughly grabbed a fistful of fur at our napes, and tossed us onto the ground. Sparks of pain lit in my left shoulder as sharp rocks dug into me. It smarted and stung, but I popped onto my feet, dusty, bruised and dazed, but okay.

Brother's rear toes splayed as they hit the ground first, as if standing on his hind legs. His back arched, to gain control, but he landed off balance. Flipping awkwardly, he came to a sudden stop by planting his muzzle on the gravel. A muffled yelp escaped, and a thin, red line trickled down his lip. Amazingly, he bounced up to face this human, who had thrown him with such anger.

Their eyes met. Brother glared intensely at the man, who did not say a word as he turned back toward the truck, gravel crunching under each foot. Brother continued to stare after him. Watching this all play out, my thoughts raced. Surely, this wasn't happening! As the man got closer to the car, the grass began to weave, the ground was moving. I felt dizzy, sick, and heavy, like my heart and head had cracked open simultaneously.

"This is not possible. People do not leave dogs," were my only thoughts.

The car door swung open with a creaking sound. The man plopped down heavily on the seat, and slammed the door behind him. The groan of the truck started and began to leave.

I was howling, running after the cloud of dust kicked up from the ground. My heart raced as dust blew into my muzzle, nose, and eyes. The man, horrible as he was, was our last connection to Mama. Not even an hour ago, we were warm and sleepy, and now? Where were we? Where was Mama?

Breathing hard, I finally slowed to a lope, then to a stop. Brother had been yelling at me as the truck pulled away, and now I heard him clearly: "We will never catch him!"

He came up beside me and sat down in the road.

"The man will not come back," he said simply.

The dust cloud dispersed in the distance. The hum from the engine faded into the morning sounds of the surrounding fields. All we could do was watch the landscape absorb the moment and feel our bewilderment grow. The sky was so vast above us; I felt raw and exposed, small and vulnerable; alone. The sounds of the field were soon drowned out by the rush of my rapidly beating heart. I started to shake uncontrollably. The pounding in my ears grew to a roar. I felt the urge to run. So I did; after the truck, which was now a speck in the distance. It felt good to move. But the more I ran, the farther away the speck went. Brother was fast, running next to me. Then the speck was gone, no dust, just fields.

We decided we would run until we found Mama. But it didn't take long and I was out of breath. I couldn't keep this up, and stopped.

"How about we just wait here? Maybe someone will

come by."

But brother kept running, even faster.

"Sis, I bet we can catch the scent of the truck and find her! C'mon!"

His fear scent was strong.

What was he thinking? We could not run all day. He finally stopped some distance away, and reversed direction back towards me. As he approached, I sensed anger building in him, something I had not ever felt from him.

"So what's your idea?" he conveyed.

"We stay put and see if someone comes by."

Reluctantly, he agreed, not wanting to admit he was just as tired and scared as I was.

So we waited.

But there were no cars or car sounds, only the sounds of the birds fetching breakfast, bugs flying by, and the soft breeze blowing the fields of grass around us. The morning heat of the sun was welcome, as it calmed some of my continual shivers. Brother sat, licking his sore nose and lip. I began to sniff the ground, weaving back and forth across the road, hoping to catch a scent of anything human, or dog for that matter.

As the sun climbed in the sky, the road remained quiet. A dark flying form overhead caught my attention. It was all black, circling a few times over us, its wings rocking side to side. It took a good look at us before it drifted away. Its presence was unsettling. By midday, the sun's heat grew uncomfortable. We were thirsty and needed shade, not to mention the pangs of hunger rumbling in our bellies.

Brother was growing irritable.

"I told you, we should have run after the car! I am drying up here, just waiting! What are we doing?"

He began to pace; his breath grew to a pant. No one was coming on this road, and we needed to find someone, a way back to Mama. My heart started to race with thoughts of drying up right here, or worse, being eaten alive by something.

Brother was having a hard time smelling anything other than his own blood, so it would be up to me to catch the scent of something helpful. I sniffed more aggressively. Nothing was familiar, not a hill or a tree or anything.

Thoughts of Mama weighed heavily on my heart. We had to find our way back to her! More thoughts flooded my mind, things she had taught me. At first it was comforting, but it fast grew to chaos. It became too hard to think, so I began to react to my surroundings.

My anxious pacing crossed over the scent of a mouse; that trail led me up to the top of a small rise near the road. The view was not much different from below, but the smells sure were! I sat and waited as small breezes brought me information. Water, food, Mama, or human—was what I was sniffing for. The first scent to hit was water. I caught a moist smell; it was faint but definitely water. Slowly, I wandered through the tall grasses, guided by the moisture-scented breeze. It took me over another rise and into a field with some jagged, wire fencing. Brother caught up to me.

"Where are you going?"

"I think water is beyond here."

"Are you sure? How do you know? We are lost out here!"

"I am not sure how far, but this is the right direction." I replied calmly.

He was panicked, and his panic was almost contagious. Without a sense of smell, he was feeling more scared than I was. I had to ignore him, trust my nose and lean into the scent.

We carefully ducked under the wire and waded into the field. I continued to track back and forth, and sure enough, the scent was getting stronger. I came across a big metal thing partially hidden by the grass. Nearby, water had puddled in some car tracks running through the clay. It was fresh, as if it had just been poured there. I was a little confused by this, to be out in the open, with cool, fresh water, but we drank heartily, regardless. Our bellies were soon full of water that had never tasted so good!

Then the big metal thing started to rumble, and water sprayed everywhere! We were getting soaked! Our fears of drying up were over! We hopped and skipped in the water, so happy to be cooling off. The joy of the moment broke our panic. The cool of the water calmed us both. We decided to wait just out of range of the spray, dry off in the sun, and see if any humans would show up. But over the slow course of the day, the only activity was the metal spraying thing and a few crickets hopping and flying nearby.

The sun was well into its afternoon heat, and my all-black fur was getting hotter by the minute. I needed shade more than water. Toward one side of the field, a low, distant hill offered a group of old trees. Shade.

Water had led us to shade. These were the only large trees to be seen, and we happily bounded over to them. But as we got closer, I let out a squeal of delight—I smelled Mama! Mama was here! I smelled her!

"She's here! She's here!"

Brother was incredulous. I ran around, sniffing the ground. Her scent was everywhere. Was she waiting for us? I excitedly ran around each of the trees, looking and sniffing the ground.

No, no, she wasn't here. I realized this was old scent. But so, why, why was there . . . oh. These were the trees she'd gone to when she left the house. Brother and I were at the very place she'd been in her story. This was the very place she'd hunted mice. And that meant she left from here to go home. So we should be able to find our way back to her! Brother understood immediately. We continued to run around excitedly, until we could barely stand. We were beyond tired.

As the day slipped into evening, an exhaustion washed over me. My body was a tired I had never felt before, almost an ache. The crickets were now fully chirping, and several small bats fluttered overhead, catching their dinner. We were on our own, and the night chill was growing, which only fueled our hunger.

The pale blue sky deepened to a dark blue, small points of light emerged I had never seen before. The darker the sky became, the more lights showed themselves. These must be the stars Mama had spoken of. I paused. If we'd come from those faraway lights to begin with, surely we could find our way back to Mama.

As the quiet of the evening grew around us, the feelings of the day caught up with me. It was all about Mama.

The soft, dry grass at the base of one of the trees felt like the best place to tuck in for the night. It felt safe. As I snuggled close to brother, his soft fur reminded me at least we had each other. The ground was hard though, so I kept shifting around, but eventually exhaustion won out, and my eyelids fluttered shut.

The sound of the wind rustling the dry grass woke me several times. Each time I wondered, was it an animal? A human? Being outside in the fenced yard during the daytime was one thing, but sleeping outside at night, in the open without Mama, was quite another. Every sound was unsettling, so I fought sleep, keeping an eye out for anything, and looking up at the twinkling stars above. The night sky was so vast. I was enchanted by my first experience of the dancing lights.

Brother was sound asleep, and I envied his ability to get comfortable and let things go. Whereas it took all my strength to not run into the dark night and look for Mama. We would have all day tomorrow. If I could just find her scent path, we would be together again! If I could just make it to dawn. She was out there, and we would find her. We had to find her. My heart was racing. I felt the urge to run. We had to find her! With that thought, the hairs on my back bristled.

I sat up and hesitantly looked around, unsure of what I was sensing. I hadn't caught a whiff of anything approaching and trembled as a large shape moved toward me out of the darkness. It was Brianna, her sparkling white coat glowing in the tall grass. I was again overwhelmed by her great size, her head so massive and noble. She had no scent, but was real, very real. She stopped to sit not a few body lengths from me, and gently gazed into my eyes. Her energy clear and familiar.

I had not seen the great Dire wolf without Mama present, and certainly had not seen her outside the dreamtime. Part of me thought I was dreaming because I was so tired. But no, no, I was awake. I could feel the breeze from the fields, the hard ground beneath my paws. I took a deep breath and mustered the courage to speak, but my first words were a mumble.

Finally I was able to say, "We have to find our way back to Mama. Can you help us?"

When she spoke, she spoke with her mind to my mind, but I felt it deep in my heart and soul. She spoke with feeling.

"You must find your own forever human. As a dog, you have chosen a life with humans. You must find one who will choose you, and when they do, you will know, for without one, your life will be incomplete."

I was stone silent. There was no mention of Mama in that statement. Did she not hear me? I asked again. She looked at me gravely.

"Little one, your Mama wants you free. She wants you to live a full dog life. To live the Code, you have to find your own forever human."

I was stunned by her words. This was not the plan I had in my heart at all. Not the plan at all! We had to find Mama, and fast! Didn't we? How would I explain Brianna's visit to brother? He'd never believed that I saw wolves, let alone spoke with one. And even if Brianna was right about us not looking for Mama, how was I going to find a forever human when I didn't even know where we were?

As my thoughts piled up, Brianna simply turned and gracefully walked away into the darkness, the faint glow following her, until the fields were all that remained.

The dawn sky brought me great relief. We had made it through the night, but I hadn't slept much after Brianna's visit. As I stretched my stiff body, the brilliant morning colors were just as Mama had described. But my experience of them was quite opposite of hers. My heart was weary from being up most of the night, missing her, experiencing the strangeness of the open fields. I felt less vulnerable in the presence of the trees, but the trees were not Mama.

Morning also brought the deeper reality of Brianna's visit. How were we to not look for Mama?

Brother was opening his eyes and feeling the effects of sleeping on the ground.

"Did you sleep, sis? I felt you moving around in the night."

"A little," I softly responded, unsure what to say about Brianna's visit. I defaulted to, "I'm hungry."

"Me too!"

"Mama caught mice here, maybe we can too," I said.

"I have no idea how to catch mice!"

"It beats not trying," I retorted.

"You just help us find Mama. I'll see about finding us something to eat."

I sighed. I knew he was frustrated, and he had his own way of missing her. And I decided I wasn't about to give up on finding Mama. Brianna's words had been clear, but I wanted Mama to be the one to convey those words to me, then I would believe them.

Brother scratched his side with his back leg and headed towards the field for water. I followed, trying to potty along the way, but not much was coming out. We needed to drink more today.

I got excited again as I smelled Mama's scent in the grass. But then I would lose it, and search to find it again. One scent trail led into the field shaded by the trees, then ended. Frustrated, I rejoined brother for another drink. I was scared to tell him about the visit from Brianna. It was hard enough for me to believe what she said. It didn't make any sense.

We both drank heavily. The water was fresh and cool and eased my dry throat. The heat was already overtaking the morning, so back to the trees we went. Determined, I quickly sniffed all around the tree rise, seeking Mama's scent. One trail led into the next, and when I lifted my nose from the ground, I realized I had been going around and around, not in any one direction. This was not going to be easy. I shared with brother that Mama had been hunting here and returning to the trees. But there had to be one scent trail which would lead us away and back to the house to Mama.

Brother was not having any luck catching mice for us. In fact, he couldn't smell them to begin with, let alone look for signs to follow them. We were both frustrated and beyond hungry. The heat was stifling; my black coat absorbed more than brother's. I was ready to get in the shade. We waited for the metal spraying thing to come on, got soaked, then went back for a snooze under the trees. This time, I fell fast asleep.

I woke to a late-afternoon sky, a light breeze pushing the warm air around, and got going. This time on my search, I wasn't in such a panic. It felt methodical. I eventually came across a scent path of Mama's that led further away from the trees than all the rest, so I kept following. At one point I flushed a quail, and later, several mice, but I was not hunting, I was searching.

I kept following until the trees we were staying at looked very far away. This had to be the path! I would have kept going, but I needed to get brother, and the sky was turning deeper evening blue. Tomorrow I would know where to go and we would follow the trail further.

As I turned back, Brianna's words kept repeating over and over in my head. A human? I was supposed to find a human? Not Mama? Humans had shown a variety of behaviors. Although Mama had shared her mama's good experiences, and her own for that matter, with the human family she was raised in. I wasn't convinced though; we wouldn't be out here on our own if it wasn't for a human.

Back at the trees, brother was grumpier than ever, having not caught anything but more hunger pangs. But as I shared the news of the scent trail, his mood softened. He too was excited at the thought of us getting closer to Mama. After going hungry for the second day, and realizing he probably would not be able to catch us any food, we were hopeful I had found the right path.

As we settled into the comfort of the largest tree for the evening, the stars emerged one by one. I felt a little less scared than the night before. I wondered if Brianna would come back. I wondered if the strange sounds would keep me up. I was so hungry—that would definitely keep me awake for a while. But one thought kept me restless long into the night. If my life wouldn't be complete without a human, how would I find the right one?

Sleep was slow to come, but when it did, my dreams were of golden fields. I was wading through them, running this way and that, searching for Mama's scent. I was hot. I was thirsty. The trees were cool. The trees were safe. The breeze cooled me and moved the branches. The scents and smells were becoming familiar. The fields gave homes to mice and rabbits, the trees gave us shade, the sun and water nourished all that was here. I was no longer a stranger within this landscape; I was learning how it was all one.

I woke with a deep impression of my surroundings in my soul. This place was teaching me who it was. The pulse of the day, the heat, the cool evenings, the stars, the night, were becoming a part of me. A sense of calm began to grow; not everything was new anymore.

Although my body was stiff, and my sleep broken, the sunrise brought me great joy. It was like the one Mama described. The patches of white in the sky were changing into reds, pinks, and oranges. The whole morning was changing color.

Brother was enjoying the morning too, although I could hear his belly rumbling, which then reminded my belly it was hungry. We were still lost and needed food. After drinking as much water as I could hold, I started down Mama's scent path, determined. Many different scents had mingled within the morning dew, and I did my best to focus on the trail I'd found yesterday. But a new scent was on Mama's path, and I came across a fresh lump of scat that hadn't been there yesterday. I stopped to take in the information. But as the hairs on my back began to stiffen, I knew—coyote. I scanned around. I could not see or smell anything new, and so went on ahead, cautious, nervous.

As I continued, I began to relax, feeling excited Mama's scent was consistent. Yes, this had to be the path! I looked back toward the trees to see where brother was. The trees looked much smaller than yesterday. I was getting more excited and kept going until I saw movement up ahead. I paused, but whew! It was only a jackrabbit running through the field. Funny looking creatures, truly. But Mama had said they were tasty. As I watched the rabbit hop away into the tall grass, I felt the urge to chase it, when my ears perked up at another sound, coming from the same direction as the rabbit. But the grass was crunching this time, and instinct told me to get low. Whatever it was, it was bigger than a rabbit.

I saw him before he saw me, but he had smelled me before I smelled him. He had the advantage of wind direction. He was a Brianna-like creature, but much smaller and thinner. Rusty browns and grays mottled his fur, giving him a rough look, but he carried it all with great confidence. But it wasn't the same noble confidence of Brianna or Mama; it was more of a dirty confidence. As if he had the ability to think one way and act another. He was a coyote.

Our eyes met. Fear coursed through me. A lot was going on behind those eyes. To pounce, to wait, to talk, to sit—I saw him biting my belly. The safety of trees was far away, and I was not sure what to do as his eyes probed me. I now knew what the rabbit felt like.

"You are alone, aren't you, little one?"

How was his voice in my head?

I didn't answer.

"I can keep you safe, and walk you back to the trees

where you and your brother are staying."

How did he know where my brother and I were staying?

I heard Mama's voice in my head: coyotes, they are not to be trusted. I began to back away, cautiously retreating through the tall grass. I heard a chilling call, and another, and another; I had never heard such chilling sounds. They found my fear, and now it flooded through me.

His friends had found breakfast.

"I better get back before nothing is left. Until next time, little one."

I trembled as he slunk away through the grass, peeing right where I was. The last drop was barely out and I ran fast through the grass, past the scat, back to the trees.

Still chasing mice, brother had worked his way towards me along the scent path. His ears were back, on full alert as we ran towards each other.

"Did you hear those calls?" he wanted to know.

"Coyotes!"

I relayed the whole story to him, word for word. I was breathless and trembling

"We have to go now!" I said.

We were both already hot, panting, craving shade. The sun was climbing in the sky and beginning its daily simmering of the fields. We couldn't stay here, but I wasn't sure where to go. A few moments passed and we hadn't moved. The hunger pangs kicked in, and we both knew if we didn't get some food, it wasn't going to matter, and we certainly didn't want to be someone else's food.

"Are you sure he was on Mama's path?" brother asked. "Maybe we should just go that way?"

"He has friends," I reminded him. "I am sure they are headed back that way now. And then they will come here."

He was not convinced, as the cries had come from a different direction than the scent trail led, so I risked going back a little ways and showed him the scat.

"This was the very thing Mama had found," I explained. "They are here, we must leave."

We chose a direction and kept going. I was nervous. I

was scared. It took all my focus to not sprint wildly, forget-
ting we were the hunted ones now. Mama's scent was faint,
but I could keep on it. I couldn't see very far ahead through
the tall field, but I smelled my earlier pee mark from a ways
away, and we worked our way around the scented area,
keeping a safe distance from where I met the coyote. I soon
lost the scent. We were moving farther and farther away
from the trees and all we had come to know. Each time I
looked back, I thought I saw the coyote in the distance.

We decided to head towards a small rise to get a better
view. Once there, it was more and more fields and more rises, but no trees. The only smell was grass, no water. I headed into the wind; at least that way I could smell something.
It was very hot going. The sun was high in the sky now, and
I was losing focus. I was hoping the next rise would offer
more direction. As we crested, it did. More fields, but this
time there were houses too. And where there were houses,
there would be water!

The midday sun had made us both weary, and we had strayed from Mama's scent several rises back. We were hungry and thirsty and had to choose. Should we go back a ways and see if we could get closer to where Mama's scent got stronger again, or should we take a chance on these houses in front of us? I felt a growing ache in my chest at not being able to find Mama. For a while, I had done so well following the scent. If only the coyote had not found me. Maybe brother had been right, and we should have stuck to the scent trail. Either way, I had failed.

We sat, panting in the sun. I was growing more and more anxious. Brother licked at a burr stuck in the fur of his paw. We were too hot, too thirsty to be waiting around. Maybe we were close to where Mama was, and I couldn't smell it. A house with lots of trees caught my eye. Maybe it would have the humans I was supposed to find? At least these houses would have water. Images of water and food lightened my heart for a moment. I was sure that if we found humans, they would want brother, of course, but me? What were my chances?

I watched my poor brother lick his painful spot and got another reminder from my tummy of all the meals we had missed since the man threw us out. Maybe Brianna was right; maybe Mama didn't want us to find her. After all, we would have to escape anyway. Oh! Maybe she had escaped already! Maybe she was now looking for us! Oh my, there was so much to think about, too much to consider. I had to move.

I started running towards the nearest house. Brother followed a ways behind me, limping along. I came to a wire fence, and the grass beyond was low, even, and green and oh, my! A huge dog was on the other side.

"Hey!"

I skidded to a stop. Oh, my! It hadn't even occurred to me there would be a dog, let alone one near Brianna's size. He was all black, like me, but with long hair and a massive head, almost like Brianna's, but wider. He walked towards me.

"Aren't you a little young to be out in the fields on your own? Where is your mama?" he said with great kindness.

I was about to answer when a human called to him from the house.

"Tino!"

The big dog looked back to her, then at us.

"Come on with me. Evening is coming, and the coyotes like to check in from time to time."

That was all I needed to hear, and I slipped under the wire onto the soft green lawn. As I got closer to him, I couldn't resist, and stood on my hind legs and put my front paws on his big legs and tried to kiss his mouth. He was the first friendly dog we had ever met. Brother followed cautiously under the fence, in awe of the size of this guy.

"It's okay, we will go inside," Tino told us. "I am sure Maria will love to see some pups."

He was right. She looked elated to see us and couldn't get to us fast enough! We must have been quite the sight though, because as we got closer, she started shaking her head, her brow furrowed, with a flash of sadness, of understanding.

Tino looked down at us.

"I'm sure it wasn't your choice, little ones, to be lost out in those fields."

No, no, it wasn't, I thought, as I looked into his kind eyes and shared the images of what had happened. He exhaled softly and sat, saddened by what was conveyed. My heart began to settle in the presence of this giant gentle soul, and now the woman coming towards us was so full of love, she reminded me of dear Jessica. The kindness, the acceptance of who we were. Maybe she would want us? Maybe she was the one I was looking for?

Her expression grew worried, and I felt her compassion. We were thirsty, hungry, weary, and brother was limping. The woman knelt down and let me kiss her. I greeted her with all the energy I had left. A nice human—how lucky was that? Of course, that was how it was supposed to be I remembered. She let us love her, as she looked at brother's paw. Attentive and gentle, she seemed to know what to do.

We all walked towards the house. She took a hose from the flower area and gently let the water flow over us, working her hands through our fur to get the dust out. The water cooled me down and calmed me down at the same time. Then she had us wait outside on the porch in the shade, and returned with a metal thing in her hand. She went to brother first and started carefully trimming away the fur that held the burr.

We were weary, and just laid in a daze, drying off. Tino laid with us. Here was a dog who knew he belonged.

As I looked around, I could see big differences from where we used to live. The yard and house didn't look as old, and there were flowers of many colors. The inside did not smell weird, and I could see there was a clean bed for Tino, with his bowls laid out one next to the other. I couldn't help but drift toward those bowls.

The woman pulled out some more bowls and filled them with food for brother and me. We easily finished the small amount, I looked up at her for more. She looked back at me with great kindness, and said words I didn't know. But after I drank a whole bowl of water, I was full.

Later she set us up on the porch with Tino. She laid out a blanket over one of Tino's beds, and it was more than big enough for brother and me. It was a mild, comfortable temperature outside. The evening light was growing, and I looked over to the rise we'd crossed to get here. Was Mama there? Was Mama looking for us? My eyes kept searching and saw something moving up that way and ran to the edge of the porch. Something was out there. Maybe it was Mama! I was about to jump down and go looking, when Tino came to my side.

"Stay here, little one."

"I think my Mama's up there!" I wagged insistently.

"Just wait."

Then another form was there. And not a moment after that, the same horrible cry from the morning seared through the dusk. It was the coyotes!

"They followed you here," said Tino. "They don't bother me, but you and your brother? You were lucky. You were smart to get your brother to safety."

I hadn't seen it that way. I only saw how I had lost the path back to Mama, and that broke my heart. I was quiet, glad at least Tino was with us. As we laid down next to him, my heart felt safe, the way it did near Mama.

I had started the day believing I would find Mama, but we came upon the coyote instead. What if I had trusted the coyote? What if Mama had not shared her story? What if brother had not been able to keep up? Today was full of all these possibilities, yet here we were, safe and comfortable. I had failed to find Mama, but I knew she would be happy we were safe. I nestled into the safe fur of Tino, knowing for the first time in a long while, I would be able to sleep the whole night through.

Safely curled up on the porch, my mind drifted through the events of the day: the heat, the fear, the grass, the searing eyes of the coyote, the cool, sweet taste of water on my tongue, the longing to stay with the scent of Mama.

I fell deeper and deeper until I entered into the dreamtime, and soon found myself in the vibrant green Highlands. The greenest, softest, cool grass was all around. I let my body sink into the damp earth, feeling the gentle calm, while connecting with the passing scents. Misty clouds hung low over the surrounding hills. A slight drizzle of rain had darkened the rocks around me. The sweet smells soothed my senses. My flock, as I had come to know them, were gently grazing, and not bothered by the misty air. Their calm was my calm, and I soaked it up and let the raindrops collect on my fur. Mama was not here, nor was Brianna. This time, it was just me.

Morning came after a deep rest, and the sensation of being alone in the Highland dreamtime lingered with me. It gave me a sense of strength and belonging to know the flock had been calm with just me, but a twinge of loss at the absence of Mama.

Maria came out and saw we were all safe, and filled our bowls a little more than the day before. She petted us and talked to us sweetly while she checked on brother's paw. As I sensed her energy, I could see staying here. So could brother. We had found a good human who would take us in.

Then a car pulled into the driveway. Tino let out a "Hey there!" We all jumped off the porch and headed toward the car, with Tino in the lead. Tino was our leader, and we were following!

As a tall man got out of the car, Tino gave him a big sniff. Then we were all sniffing him, wagging around his

legs. I was singing with great delight and brother was jumping around happily. Maria made it into our greeting pack,
and began chatting with him as he reached down to greet
us.

Maria and the man chatted for a bit, while the man
petted brother. Then he called to us to get into the car. I
was confused. We were staying here with Tino, right? The
woman was nice and I liked it here.

I slinked away when the gentle man crouched down
next to us. He wanted to take us with him. No, I think we
will be staying right here, thank you. Brother at first didn't
know what to do, then he joined me in hiding behind Tino.
The man seemed nice and all, but we just got here, and we
didn't know him. So we stayed put.

He stayed crouched down and put his hands out, smiling
at us. I knew his intentions were good, but I liked it here.
He was putting in quite the effort—I felt the kindness of his
heart energy—but there was so much to leave if we got into
that car. And so much we didn't know.

The woman watched us all frozen in the moment. She
picked me up and held me close. Her eyes, conveyed the
same types of images I was getting from the man: a new
place, more dogs and a kind woman. So, she didn't want
us. But she loved us. The gentleness of the moment eased
my fears, and I let her set me on the backseat. Tino's eyes
followed as the man lifted brother in beside me. I would
miss the gentle giant, the first friendly dog I had ever met. I
kept my eyes on him, and for a brief moment he looked like
Brianna. I felt Brianna. She was there too, watching us go.

As we drove away, Austin, as he was called, rolled the windows down a bit. The warm breeze brought many smells and kept us comfy as the heat of the day was coming on. I looked out the windows with both sadness and confusion. If we hadn't found Tino's house, the coyotes would almost certainly have caught us. He and the woman had saved us, and I'd thought that meant we would have a home. The woman was nice, but she didn't want us. She already had Tino. We had found a home, yes, but it was not the home we had hoped to find. Brother looked at me. He must have felt my thoughts, for he was quite still as the car buzzed along the road.

We passed field after golden field, crossing the same distance in a few moments that had taken us a half a day to cover on our own. How full those moments had been for us: hunger, thirst, fear of being eaten, fear of not finding

Mama. Where was she? How was she? I hoped she was okay. I hoped she had escaped. I hoped she was free.

How short my time with her had been. Yet she was my focus and protection. She was the reason we'd made it out of those fields, to get back to her, and without her, I wasn't sure what I would do. The further we drove, the more sadness began to wash over me. Soon we were out of the fields and on a very busy road. The many houses seemed to fill the windows, along with green lawns and wooden fences, more cars and pavement. We were now a world away from Mama. I felt the last attempt to find her slip away. I began to tremble.

Was this what she wanted? Her two pups in some guy's backseat? Brianna had said Mama wanted us to be free. Well, I was free enough to realize I missed her immensely and to know I would probably never see her again. Brianna's words became more real to me: 'You must find your own forever human,' as in for always. We had to find a new Jessica, or a Maria, but one who wanted us. For it was becoming more clear: one dog, one human. But wait, I wanted to stay with brother.

The car was really moving now. We looked out the windows at tall, stained wooden poles, trees, cars, signs and houses. After a few turns off the busy road, it was just houses and poles. We turned again and slowed down. Brother was alternately licking his cut lip and his paw. Austin noticed and said kind, soft words. We wagged a little, feeling his loving energy.

It wasn't long before the car pulled up to a small house with a high fence in the back. We heard several dogs calling out. I felt my empty stomach tighten; so many stories all at once. One wanted a 'walk'—what was a 'walk'? Another said she had been here for a few weeks, another was glad to be here but no one had looked at him to take him home. Wait, this wasn't his home?

Brother looked at me.

"I dunno, sis. This may not be where we want to be."

I looked back at him, my tail between my legs, tired,

sad, missing Mama, and longing for a feeling of safety.

Austin said a few words, including, 'out,' but it sounded exciting as he opened the door for us. Brother jumped right out, but I stayed on the seat. If I got out, it was one more step away from Mama.

Austin looked at me with kind eyes and started playing with brother. We were in a setting, like where Maria lived, but with more houses closer together. The dogs were calling: 'Let us out!'

Austin looked in at me.

"C'mon, sweetie," he said.

So, I jumped out, sniffed a bit, and peed on the lawn. Many dogs had peed here. I was a little slow to leave my pee spot, taking in all the scents, but Austin encouraged me to come inside, so I did. Brother was a few paces ahead of me. Inside, cardboard was on the floor that smelled of dog pee, and oh! A cat skittered to a back hallway. I stayed in the doorway, tentatively taking it all in. Many dogs had been here. Many dogs were here! What did it all mean? Brother, not the best smeller in the world, rushed to the water bowl, and started lapping it up. I followed him. Although the dish smelled like many dogs, I joined in; I was thirsty too!

I saw a tall glass window that went to the floor with two dogs looking in, wagging. Another little white one pushed her way between the legs of the bigger dogs and nosed up too. They all looked in, and we looked out at them. I sat, ears perked. Brother went closer to the glass. The little white dog kept wagging with her eyes set upon him. It was very clear she liked my brother!

We heard a car pull up to the house, and both of us gave a few 'who's that?' announcements.

Austin replied with kind words.

The front door opened, and a smiling, blonde-haired woman came in. She looked at brother and me and spoke kind words. She was so pleased to meet us I felt pulled to love her in return.

I sprinted as fast as I could and jumped up on her before she could even close the door. Brother was right behind me. I wagged my tail so hard my whole back end was moving with it. We pawed at her legs, saying.

"We love you, we love you, we love you."

The woman set her things down and scooped us both up. It felt so good to be held. We both eagerly licked her face, while Austin and the woman were talking to each other.

A lot was said, and my mind worked to keep up. Austin

called her, 'Elise,' as she put out full bowls for us and went to the table. The food was tasty, and it felt good to have full bellies for the first time in days. I padded over to 'Elise' and sat at her feet. She picked me up and set me on her lap. She was looking at a screen like the one I'd seen when we lived with Mama. As she looked, she petted my head, and I settled in, happy to be held.

As Austin chatted with her, I heard the words 'uncle' and 'brother,' and with those words, I saw my brother with an image of an older, heavy man. It was not someone we had met, yet he seemed very kind, and interested in brother.

Elise set me down on the cardboard-covered floor and said some new words to me, in a higher pitched, kind voice that grabbed my attention. I cocked my head at the words 'camera' and 'internet.' She held a small, silver object. It didn't smell like food, so I sat patiently watching her.

She was talking in that voice, with the little box aimed at me. She kept smiling, and so I sat longer, loving her back. Austin was smiling. Elise was laughing. Somehow I was making them happy by just sitting in front of the box being myself. I think I liked this camera thing.

"Good girl!" she said.

She picked me up, and hugged and kissed me and walked through the big glass. The other dogs were wagging out-side. I began to tremble—so many smells and stories. Elise bent down, still holding onto me, and let the dogs approach to sniff me. The largest one was a solid-looking dog, tawny, but with super hard muscles, a very wide head with little ears. I had never seen a dog like that.

"Jade," Elise said.

Jade put her nose out to sniff me and looked into my eyes. I saw teeth gnashing, biting and barking, and darkness. Her story scared me, and I pulled back. But then I looked back into her eyes and sent her my message: "I'm here with my brother and don't know where our Mama is. Would you like to play?" With much delight, Jade gave me a big lick. I kissed her back.

Elise set me on the ground and Jade sniffed me again. I was so happy, I jumped up with my paws on her side. She growled and snarled. I yelped and jumped back towards Elise, who tried to convey images of being too excited and letting dogs have their space. Back at Maria's house, big Tino had just stood there, letting me kiss him. I guess not all dogs were into kissing. Jade recomposed herself, looking into my eyes. "It was too much too fast."

The other dogs came around also. So I just sat and let them sniff me. It was hard to be patient and not jump up on them, but Jade had taught me to curb my enthusiasm, at least for the time being. While Jade was squat, another dog was quite old, and the little white one was very dear. She came right up to my face and gave a short 'hey'!

"Finally, someone my own size!" she exclaimed, and ran after the ball Austin was throwing for brother. The older gray dog looked down at me.

"You remind me of my sister's pup."

I looked up at him. He must have been older than Mama, much older. I wasn't sure what to think. Where had his people gone?

His name was Ted, and he explained how his humans had packed things up in boxes. A van came and loaded them all up, and he was left at the house. He waited all day and into the night. But no one came back for him. Eventually, some humans came, and put him in a metal box, and took him to a place where all dogs were kept in these metal boxes. I was stunned. Being left after growing old with humans? What was going on? So even if I found my forever people, they might not keep me forever? They might just pack their things and leave? The Code was being ignored. Did humans even follow it? I shook my head. Elise looked at me, with a question on her face.

Y'know, it's really hard hearing these stories, my eyes said. We are dogs; humans best friend. How has it come to this?

Later Austin came over with the 'camera.' I was with Jade, then with Ted, and soon the little white princess, Whitney. We were quite the odd pack. I felt sad. Was this what my life was going to be about? Living in a fenced backyard with a random pack of dogs whose humans let them go, hearing their stories of lament. Surely life would be better than this. Surely this isn't what Mama had intended for me. I stared past the fence, up into the sky.

Elise sensed my sadness coming on. Maybe she was feeling my energy. She hugged me close, and whispered assuringly. Then it occurred to me: there were no other puppies here. Maybe it wouldn't take too long to be 'adopted,' the word they kept saying. This was a new word to me, but I was starting to get the idea. I darted toward the fence, running as fast as I could round and round. I darted in and around the other dogs like they were sheep.

Jade soon joined me and we began to play-chase. She

panted heavily, prancing around me, almost ran over me, but jumped instead, pirouetted mid-air and landed facing me; and I ran into her! She just rolled over and laid down, with me next to her.

Soon all of us laid on the grass together, the way we used to with Mama. This was not my original pack, but it felt like a pack of some kind. We were a pack of dogs whose humans didn't want us.

I was hot after all that running and went over to what looked like a water dish. Sure enough, fresh water was being pumped in continuously. After my drink, I stood there, looking around. This wasn't so bad.

Elise picked me up to bring me inside. I wasn't sure why I had to come in. She spoke to me in a certain tone and I knew a few of the words, like 'inside.' I now learned 'safe,' connecting it to the moment when Jade had snarled at me and Elise picked me up. So I relaxed in her arms, knowing where I was going and why.

We sat down at the table, in front of the screen she called 'the laptop.' Austin handed her a little black square, and she stuck it into the side of the laptop. I looked at the screen when light started to dance on it.

It was brother! I leaned forward in her lap to get a better look. But who—who was that next to him? After a moment I figured out it was me! I am all black with some white on my chest and rear toes.

'Images' of dogs I had never seen before started to appear. There were more and more and more, moving up and disappearing, then more and more and more, and, oh, a cat!

The screen showed many, many, many, many, many dogs and cats. Many looked like me, some like Jade and Ted and Whitney, and some that looked like a little bit of each of us, but in one dog! How did all those images get there? Did this mean there were more places like here? I leaned into Elise's belly. There were just so many of them; where were all their people? I looked out to the yard. My new pack was all at the glass, looking in at us. Jade connected with my eyes. I tried to convey, but the concept was beyond comprehension. How many of 'us' were there?

Maybe it was the long day we'd had or what I had just seen on the laptop, but the last thing I remember is Elise placing me softly on the bed where she and Austin slept. I woke much later to a darkened room, disoriented, not knowing where I was. But as my eyes adjusted and my nose pulled in information, I realized I was still on the bed in between Elise and Austin, with brother next to me. We were safe. I wondered if Mama or Brianna knew how many dogs needed to find their people. To make matters more difficult, I was some kind of mix between two dogs—who would want that? All those faces pleading, so many, so many. I began to get worked up and almost jumped off the bed.

"The people are looking for you too, you know."

Startled, I turned towards the voice. It was Brianna, standing at the far side of the room. My first thought was she did not understand just how many dogs needed to find people. Plus I was not the 'type' people were looking for. I knew that firsthand. And here was beat-up Jade, old Ted, and the white princess Whitney, all on their second search for humans.

"And yet there was Tino, and your Mama's family, and all the dogs with loving humans before you," Brianna said.

"But do you know how many have not found their humans? And now humans are leaving us!"

She lowered her head.

"The Code is being broken, there is no doubt. But we are the Code. It is not a choice for us; it's who we are."

The morning light came early. I stretched with the soft feeling of sleep still wrapped around me. I realized both Elise and Austin were on the edges of the bed, and during our sleep brother and I had filled in the space between. As they woke, hugs and love were showered over each of us. I sank deeper into the blankets, and soaked it up.

After a bit we jumped down from the bed and followed Austin out into the hall. He opened a door near the food place which led to a tidy room with bright morning light streaming in from two small, high windows. It had a dog-sized door opening out to the fenced backyard. The far wall had dog beds lined up next to each other, one for each dog, although Whitney and Ted slept in the same bed. Jade was right next to them.

Elise followed us into the garage. Food bowls were filled, stretching was happening, tails were wagging, and Elise hugged and kissed each and every dog. As I watched

Elise with them, I felt a stirring in me and saw a soft light around them. It felt peaceful.

We all went out to the backyard for the morning potty. Elise picked up brother and held him close. He kissed her all over her face. "I love you, Elise," he was saying.

Austin said kind words to brother. I watched, but grew worried as I picked up a scent. I had smelled this scent before; this was very familiar - when Cindy went away. I looked up at Austin and whined and pawed at his legs. This had to do with the gentle man I saw through Elise.

"Wherever he goes, I go."

Elise sat down on the grass and picked me up, so brother and I shared her lap. She looked deep into my eyes. I stared back and saw her dilemma. They only wanted my brother.

She squeezed us both tight before setting us down on the grass. A fly flew right by my head, and I lunged after it. I chased it until it flew high over the fence. When I stopped and looked back, Elise had gone.

We were all out in the yard, as the morning was not too hot. I was taking in the smells, the sounds of being with my new friends. Being outside was calming. To feel the air and sun on my fur gave me a sense of peace.

Austin was sitting at the table on the deck. Jade was next to his chair, looking over at me. Ted was fast asleep in the grass and brother was sniffing around with Whitney. My survey was interrupted by some muffled tones from inside the house. I didn't know what it was, but Jade sat up to announce. So I followed her lead.

"Who's there? Who is that!"

Austin praised our announcement, as he walked to the big glass. Whitney followed with some exuberant yaps, and Ted woke up and followed our words with his own "Hey!" We all watched Austin go inside and close the glass door behind him. Another man was inside. They were talking, and soon both stepped out into the yard.

The man was older, balding, and had a little bit of a belly. I put it together; this must be 'uncle.' He saw brother, and called to him. We all came running. I sensed he was a follower of the Code by the way he rubbed up Ted's belly with one hand, and scratched Jade's back with the other. He was smiling and happy to see all of us.

The man was very good-natured, and Austin was very comfortable with him, which meant he was in Austin's pack. This set us both at ease, as brother was very comfortable with Austin. But the man's energy was focused towards brother, not me, and that gave me an uneasy feeling.

He cheerily called over to brother again.

Brother was wagging at the warm and welcoming attention directed his way. So he let uncle pick him up and hold him close.

Uncle continued saying caring words to brother.

Brother looked back at me. I could see he was happy but also worried. He squirmed to be let go, to get to me. I ran to uncle's feet and sat perfectly, ears fly way, and conveying he should also take me. I even gave him a short pawing to emphasize my intent. He let brother down and we sat together, looking back up at him.

He was smitten with brother, but not with me. And instantly I was sad. Austin sensed my distress and reached out for me, but instead of letting him hold me, I darted away to escape the feeling. Brother followed me and sat very close to me.

"He seems nice enough, sis, and he really likes me. We can't stay here forever, right?"

It wasn't about staying here, it was about never seeing brother again, of us not being together in this life, it was about our plan to all be together not happening. The same feeling we had now about Mama.

I watched as brother slowly walked away from me. The last of my own pack was leaving. I ran after him, caught up and playfully pinned him in the grass, licking his face all over. He lovingly licked me back. For a moment, we were pups again, with Mama next to us, the smell of milk on her fur, and its sweet taste on our lips. It was sunny and warm and we knew nothing but joy. Then we were back in the yard, on the grass with Austin and uncle, with the other dogs looking at us as we said good-bye.

I watched as uncle carried brother through the glass door. He looked back at me, and my gaze remained on him until I could no longer see his eyes.

After a few moments, I heard a car door bang shut. And a car hum started in the driveway. My heart sank further as the sound grew and then faded away, along with the scent of brother. He would not be coming back. My sisters, my Mama, and now my brother were all gone. Had Brianna known all along? Had Mama known my life would come to this? Without realizing it, my nose pointed to the sky and a slow, sorrowful song began. The sound built from deep inside, as I sang with the pain of many dogs before me, going back, going back, all the way to Brianna.

Jade came and sat next to me. I kept howling, the sounds and tones coming from deep within, until they were all said. She bent down and licked the top of my head with one solid lick. I looked up at her big block of a head, with a jaw that could have eaten me up in one bite, and felt comforted. She looked back with gentle eyes and licked me again.

It was getting towards midday, and I hadn't moved. Jade had stayed right next to me the entire time. I realized all the dogs had felt the pain of my song. They had all been hurt in this way, and were all looking for their second or third humans now. There were no brothers or sisters or mamas around, so my song was a song for all of us. The sadness we all carried yet were so willing to let go of for the lighter moments, for yet another chance at love.

Austin had been watching me, concern on his face.

Then he stood up with excitement and said the word, 'park,' a few times.

I had never heard the word 'park' before, but Jade and Whitney flew happily at Austin, even Ted raised his head and pulled his aging body up by his front legs. His soft groan saying, "I'm coming too." It must have meant something good.

I knew they all wanted to do it, but I sat and watched,

feeling the excited energy around me, but not knowing what it was about. Jade looked back at me. I felt the pull of her expression.

"It'll do you good to move. C'mon, little one."

Austin opened the gate in the fence which led to the street. I didn't want to be left behind, so I sprinted after my group of dogs. We all ran out, tails wagging.

"Why are we this excited?" I asked.

"You'll see!" Whitney replied.

Austin was walking towards a big tan car with a big door he slid open. There were no seats, just a big space. Jade was the first one in, jumping strongly and landing with a thud. Whitney sproinged in from a standing position, landing lightly. She could really jump! I ran and jumped as hard as I could, landing awkwardly, sliding into the side of Jade's leg. She whipped around and snarled. Those teeth and huge mouth flashed towards me. I closed my eyes, waiting for I didn't know what! But she stopped just short of touching me.

"Sorry, little one, old habits."

I opened my eyes as she licked my head. Her gentle nature was hidden behind her toothy smile. I knew it as a smile, but I feared others saw it as a snarl.

Ted was the last one to the van. As Austin helped him in, we made space by the door. Ted grimaced as he sat.

"Oh, I hate riding in this thing, but it's what's on the other side that gives me joy."

The door slid shut, bang! I leaned on Jade for comfort, and she let me. Austin hopped in front, and we were moving. All the dogs stayed near the front, and I soon found out why. Cool air was blowing, and you could see where we were going. Jade let me sit in front of her so I could look out.

It ended up being a short trip. As the door opened, I was overwhelmed by a massive waft of scent from the all dogs outside. Austin helped Ted get out, then we all followed. Through a criss-cross wire fence I could see too many dogs to count, running and jumping and playing with their people and each other. As we got closer, fear welled up in me seeing this many dogs all at once, and I slowed to the rear of our pack.

I had never been around so many different-looking dogs. Every size, shape and color were all running around together: long fur, short fur, black, white, tan, many colors, two colors, tall, short, thick, and thin. I looked for Mama and brother. Mama wasn't here, but there were many dogs who looked kind of like her, and even one that looked like a bigger version of brother. How was this all possible? Then I thought about Mama's story. Of course, it was possible! I started to feel not so out of place.

But there were just so many, so many stories, and the pace was so fast. They all looked like they were having fun, but I wasn't sure I would have any fun.

Jade ran over to a few dogs, who wagged as they saw her coming. Whitney saw a short, wiry, energetic little guy and ran towards him. Ted lumbered towards the row of humans standing along the fence.

"Those are the humans of my dog friends," he softly mentioned to me. He missed his own humans so much, and these people loved seeing him.

Which left me, standing by myself, watching all that was happening in the fenced area. I sat and watched, looking for brother again, but he was not here. I wasn't sure what to do. Austin squatted down beside me.

He spoke to me in his kind and understanding tone, and petted me. Then he encouraged me to follow him, and so I did. I had not taken but a few steps when a fuzzy yellow ball rolled by me. I lunged for it, and was bringing it over to Austin. Before I knew it, two dogs were on me, growling.

"Give it back! That's our ball!"

One nipped me on the right flank; I yelped! From out of nowhere, Jade ran towards me with great speed. The full force of her solid body plowed into the dog who had bitten me. He flew against the fence; the other was flattened to the ground. The first one slunk back over to us, meekly saying, "It's our ball."

Jade shot back a snarl.

"You can ask nicely. She's just a pup, and it's her first time here."

"Wanna push it with me?" asked the second dog.

Jade issued a deadly snarl, and both dogs left, grumbling. Austin rushed over to us. His face and tone showed great concern and disdain at the same time. He pet Jade affirmingly. I realized he was thanking her, and as for me, he picked me up and held me close, gently feeling the side where I'd been nipped.

I'd never been bitten before and had never met such mean dogs. Austin looked me over, saying some words of lightness and safety. He grabbed the ball, and threw it back.

A man came walking towards us, saying words in a harsh, loud manner. His tones were not unlike the man who had dumped brother and me. To my surprise, gentle Austin's energy got big and angry to match, but was protective, like Mama would have been. He set me down, and I hid under Jade's belly.

The other man's face changed after Austin finished his words. His energy shrunk down. Austin sternly said a few more words, then the man called for his dogs and walked away.

Jade stayed with me while my heart slowed to a normal beat. It occurred to me this was what she was used to doing—fighting with other dogs, although it wasn't in her nature to be aggressive. Yet thankfully, she felt protective of me. She was kind at heart. Surely someone would see that and take her home with them.

This was turning out to be quite a day! I wished brother were here with me. Austin picked me up and held me close. His words were so kind. I heard 'little girl' and knew he was conveying safety. He petted me and kissed my head. I pressed myself against his chest, soaking up the comfort.

One of the other dogs came over to us; her human was right behind her. This dog looked like a bigger version of brother. Austin looked down at her smiling.

"Hi, Tina!" he said.

Tina wagged at being engaged in conversation. Jade gave her a few gentle sniffs. I peered down from Austin's arms and saw that Tina's eyes were soft but playful. I wriggled to get closer, and Austin gently lowered me down to Tina's level. She licked my face, then stretched both front paws out on the ground, with her butt in the air, tail wagging. She was saying, "I like you. Let's play!"

No one besides brother had ever asked me to play before, so "Okay!"

I jumped out of Austin's arms, as Tina took off into the fray of dogs. I took off after her! She was zigging and zagging, and really flying around the park. I was chasing her with all of my speed, my body fluid and nimble. This was more like it!

Tina would stop and freeze, then jump in the air, then start again. Then we'd both stop, panting, then lie down, then roll on our backs in the grass. We played like this until I could barely see straight, and my tongue was hanging out farther than it ever had. Running felt so good. I felt so joyous and alive as I padded back over to Austin. Tina was panting right behind me. We laid down together at Austin's feet.

His grin was as wide as I had seen it. He was happy for me. I was happy for me! This was the most fun I'd had since I'd been a little pup, playing in the yard with Mama and my brothers and sisters.

Austin said something that made Tina's human laugh. She was looking at Tina with such a big smile and with such care. It was not unlike Mama's look with us. I watched Tina get up and dance around her human mama. The love and warmth in the face of her human; how Tina felt being petted and hugged and loved. How she leaned in to get more, and soaked it all up. I saw a glow deepen around each of them; they were together, within the glow. It was so much like the feeling of being loved by Mama, but now I was seeing it between another dog and a human! The energy was making me giddy. I realized; they were their own pack—a dog and a human!

My blood rushed. I saw things through Mama's eyes. The human who had cared for Mama's mama, the loving bond that had been shared. The agreement that had been kept. How dog and human loved one another as a pack. I saw my own life as many lives going backwards, one after the other, one long connection with humans. The bond to humans was true. This was what I was looking for; this was the feeling. Brianna was right! It was real.

Once home, we all hopped out and made our way to the backyard. Ted brought up the rear, with his lumbering gait. Austin used the hose to rinse the obvious dirt from white Whitney, and I got another drink of water from the ever-flowing fountain of fresh water. Jade was right behind me.

After we drank, we laid up on the deck. The sun was shining, the air was warm, and my black fur was warming in the sun, lulling me into a snooze. I stretched out on my side, legs out, and fell softly into a deep sleep . . . The mean dog was hitting the fence, Jade was snarling, the ball tasted yucky, but I liked the smell. I dropped the ball. I was running, watching the back end of Tina and following her tail. I saw Whitney prancing with two reddish dogs. I rolled and stopped, then Tina ran by me, taunting me, so I shot up to catch her. I ran harder and harder, Mama was there, she smiled and sissy was gone, brother was gone, and I yelped to say hello and they were going away, and I yelped again and ran and ran and they were gone.

I woke suddenly and looked around. I was still in the backyard. Jade was sprawled out a few body lengths away, white Whitney was peeing out on the grass, and Austin was nearby, talking on the phone. Mama was not here, nor sissy, or brother, but I was not alone. Jade eventually came over and laid down next to me. She was sunning herself and seemed more peaceful than before we'd gone to the park. I sensed Jade had had many frightening encounters in her life, and every time she ran, she left a few of them behind.

Austin's phone beeped. He looked over at Jade and said some words to her. His smile, and tone were explanatory, someone was coming to see her. Jade's ears perked up at hearing her name, but she was too comfy to move and just laid there, softly blinking her eyes. I noticed dark lines on her hide, where her fur was missing. There was one, then another, and another, and still more on one side. Some were like dots, others a little longer. I put it together; they were scars from her days of fighting and I was sure each one had a painful memory. No wonder she didn't want another dog touching her. Oh, Jade, I hope you find someone as loving as Tina's mom!

A man showed up, and Austin let him in through the gate. He seemed nice enough, but Jade was not into meeting him. She stayed put and growled from the deck.

When Austin said to come, she stood where she was, then laid back down.

Austin sighed.

"Hold on," he said to the man.

I ran over to the visitor and greeted him with a wagging body and tail. He said "Hey, little pup," and patted me on the head roughly. I didn't like being patted on the head—it hurt! I slunk away like I was going to pee as Jade was still quietly growling. The man put the white smoking thing in his mouth, something I remembered and did not like from the house where I grew up. Austin noticed too. A few moments passed, and he walked back towards the man. They both looked over at Jade a few times, while chatting, then Austin shook his hand, and the man left, closing the gate behind him.

Well, clearly finding a forever human wasn't as easy as someone just showing up. Austin petted Jade lovingly on her block head. She knew who she didn't like, and that man was someone she didn't like. The cues he gave resonated with her sense of what wasn't safe. Austin must have agreed, because he did not force her to do anything.

He went into the house and came back out with a tall, thin box in his hands. His hand was in the box, making a certain crinkle sound. Jade perked up; so did Whitney. Ted was sound asleep on the other end of the deck, but as Austin's hand rustled in the box, his head popped up. They were all looking at the box in Austin's hands, so I did too.

Austin gave each of us one. Jade got two. It was crunchy and meaty. We were all crunching together, crumbs falling out of everyone's mouth onto the deck, but we lapped those up, leaving wet areas, which the sun quickly evaporated .

Not long after our 'treat,' we heard another car pull up to the front of the house. A car door shut, then another. Two people were getting out. Jade gave a quick, 'Who's that?' as Austin started to walk towards the gate. This time a woman and a girl walked in. The woman reminded me of Tino's mom and the older girl was sad but strong. Jade studied the new people from her vantage on the deck, but she did not growl.

Austin invited them in; he was smiling.

Jade heard her name and focused more intently. While Austin was talking to the them, the daughter could not take her eyes off of Jade. A minute later, Austin called for Jade. She just sat there, sniffing the air.

The girl crouched down and put out her hand.

She asked for Jade softly.

Jade liked being asked things, not told things, and this girl was asking. The girl's gentleness softened Jades initial resistance to connect. Slowly, she walked towards them and then sniffed the girl's hand. The girl just stayed crouched down, motionless, and let Jade come closer to her.

The girl was very shy, and her energy was kind to be sure, but I sensed something else in her. Something I had not sensed in a human. Yet it was familiar; it was hurt. It was pain.

I watched Austin look over Jade. He looked at her scars, her lopsided ear, her broken toe and watched the girl stroke her scars and her ear. Jade quivered, and I started to see the glow. Austin's face softened; he saw Jade getting some real love from someone who saw her for who she was.

Austin spoke to the girl calmly, and she smiled and start-ed petting Jade all over. I understood by Austin's tone that Jade was going leave us next. I licked her face, and Jade gave me one big lick back. It said all I needed to know.

The shadows grew on the lawn as the sun dropped and disappeared behind the nearby houses. The air softly cooled. Jade was gone from us now, and the fenced yard felt much bigger without her. Our unlikely friendship would be dearly missed, and I knew I probably would never see her again, which added tingles of sadness to the sadness already pooled around my heart. I closed my eyes and rested my head on the deck. She had hopefully found her human in that loving girl, and knowing that was helping to keep my heart above water. Jade had protected me at the park, just like Mama would have. If it hadn't been for Jade, those dogs would have rolled me hard or worse. Her leaving opened up so many worries in me. I was now without a friend and alone. I was scared and felt uneasy about what would happen to our little pack. Who would protect us? Who would leave? What new dog would be coming?

I settled in near Ted, as I had not gotten to know him

yet. He began to share more details of how he came to be here with Austin and Elise. After his people left him alone, other people found him in the neighborhood. He was taken to a place with many types of dogs in metal boxes—so many boxes. It stunk, was loud and brightly lit all day long. They had to pee and poo in their own cage, as being let out was not often. The people tried to take care of them all, and they got to go outside for brief moments of time, but none of the dogs were happy. In fact, they were very miserable.

Ted was overwhelmed by the anguish of the dogs in the 'cages', as the humans referred to them. Surely being in a cage was some type of misunderstanding. If they were let out, they could find their way back to their humans. With all of that tormented energy, the dogs weren't able to show their true selves to the people coming by. So as people would come, he said, sometimes a dog would go away with them, but most of the time the people just kept walking. Every time he heard the room door open, he hoped it would be his people. But it never was.

Then one morning, certain dogs were let out of their cages and taken through a door towards the back of the room. The first dog had shown a slight sense of joy at being let out, but the second dog resisted. The humans stuck him with a needle and dragged him out as he went limp. Soon half the cages were empty, and Ted never saw those dogs again. He sensed something very wrong had happened.

Later, people came and gave each cage a thorough cleaning. By the end of the day, the cages that had been emptied were once again full of scared dogs. Ted tried to make sense of this. The next day, during an outside potty trip, a gate in the yard had been left open, and Ted saw a pile of black plastic bags being loaded into a large truck. One of the bags was open, and he saw the stiff legs of a dog who had been across from his cage; Ted wet himself.

Dogs in cages? Dead dogs in bags? I felt nauseous.

"How did you make it here, Ted?" I asked with the softest energy.

The morning he'd seen the bags, Elise had walked through the cage room. She crouched down and put her hand through the wire. Ted saw her eyes and lumbered over. She'd seen his sadness and said words to the man who brought the dogs in and out. She brought Ted home with her that very day.

He was grateful to be alive after what he had seen and been through, and he wanted everyone to know it, especially Elise and Austin.

"I know you are so young to know this, but we all must know what is really going on with the humans," Ted shared.

My eyes drifted away into thought. He felt my worry about being taken to a place like that. He had seen several pups come and go in his time here, he said, and I shouldn't worry too much, as the humans were all too eager to cuddle a puppy.

While Austin was in the food place, getting food ready, I heard Elise's car pull up. He saw me running for the big glass and cheerfully opened it so I could dash inside. He spoke to me in the certain voice he had for us, and I picked out the words 'car,' and 'Elise.'

"Why yes, yes, exactly!" I conveyed with my eager eyes and squeals of delight.

I ran right past him to the front door. My goal: to greet her as she came in! I still had Elise, and she was my friend. I sang excitedly, paws dancing and tail wagging with great anticipation as the door opened. As my eyes connected with hers, the louder I sang.

"I'm here. I missed you. I love you. You saved Ted. I am so glad you are here. I am so glad you came back!"

Her smiled widened into "Hi, little girl!"

She had a large brown paper bags in her arms. Food smells wafted out of each and deeply into my nose: bread, chicken, eggs, vegetables, and something very fragrant. Of course, I knew it wasn't for me, but I was always eager to see what was inside those bags that smelled of food.

She set the bags on the counter. I followed behind her and sat at her feet. She bent down to pick me up, and I licked her face eagerly.

"Love you. So glad you are home!"

She held me close, and I snuggled into her arms. I found such great comfort nestling under her chin. Still carrying me, she picked up the laptop and walked out to the table on the deck. Austin followed with a couple drinks in hand.

Elise was nodding and excited about something she was reading on the screen. Austin was leaning in to see and their discussion included my name several times. Their energy was light. Her face kept changing. I studied her, and for moments at a time, I sensed she was seeing me with various people. I knew what she was doing. It was what she'd done with brother and then Jade; she was deciding on a human for me. She was looking for my human!

As I watched Austin and Elise converse, I felt relaxed and settled inside; a part of their conversation and shared energy. Connecting with humans was possible, and felt very similar to connecting with Mama, or brother, or Jade for that matter. Elise communicated with me through her feelings and images. I now felt peace. They were looking after me, caring for me. No, they couldn't keep me, but they were finding someone who could. This was the Code. This is what Brianna and Mama had been trying to tell me, but telling does not compare to knowing, and now I knew.

The next thing I remembered was waking up on their bed in the morning. They were still asleep, but the morning light was coming up and the birds were chirping. I plopped down and went to look through the big glass. Pink and blue hues filled the sky; it was a beautiful morning, like the mornings brother and I spent back at the trees. My thoughts drifted to brother and Jade and, of course, Mama. Lost in the moment, I was startled when Elise called out to me.

Her voice was animated, talking to me in the way that let me know it was about me. She was all about let's "get going" and "getting ready!" She and Austin were very excited, so something good was happening, and we were going to do it! After food for all, a quick potty, and a 'good morning' to Ted and Whitney, we were out the door.

The drone of the road noise and warmth of the car lulled me into a droopy-eyed on and off snooze. The ride kept going, but eventually we slowed and pulled off the busy road. Elise had held me on her lap the whole way. Now I sat up to see where we were stopping. Through the windows, the trees were leafy and green, and a light breeze was blowing them. The sky was cloudy but bright. The paved road we were on curved into a gravel one which led to a small flat area. It was some kind of 'park', kind of like the dog park, but without a fence and a few weathered tables. Austin found a spot and the car stopped moving.

Elise was gently petting my ears and back. Every touch told me she loved me. The energy of her hands was warm and light, but deep with meaning. It was comforting, but I couldn't help feel a little fear now that we were here, as there were no people around. We sat in the car, looking out, and Elise reassured me all would be well. Her words were kind, her tone was explanatory, and I caught glimpses of the human she was imagining for me.

She opened the door, set me down and I started sniffing around. So many scents to take in: rats, mice, dogs and many birds. I enjoyed following a scent trail into the grass. We'd waited for a little bit when a car pulled in next to ours. Elise became elated and called for me!

This was the moment. My ears perked up; I was alert to who was in that car. I could see a woman waving at us from inside. Was it true she was excited to see me? As she stepped out, she felt very similar to Elise; she was calm, kind, and had the biggest grin on her face. She was speaking so fast and so happily—and she was talking to me! I wiggle walked over to her as fast as I could.

"Hello, hello, hello!" this is me!

She crouched down and let me love her all over, kisses and all! I was wiggling so much she could barely pet me, but when I felt her hands on me, I felt great warmth and kindness.

She shook hands with both Elise and Austin. I heard them say 'hi Olivia.' They acted at ease with her. Elise asked me to 'sit.' I understood the concept, and so I did my best to contain myself, squirming in place.

Olivia's face lit up with surprise. She praised me instantly, saying "good sit." She kept petting me. Oh, she felt good. She was gentle and kind and looked so deeply into my eyes. I stared back excitedly. She was really looking; she wanted to see me! I felt warm inside, like when Mama used to look at me, asking me how I was, seeing all of me.

I wanted to know who Olivia was. Gazing at her, I saw glimpses of sadness, pain, joy, a forest, happiness and arguing. Much the way Jade held pain, I could see a life made up of events and feelings, all present, yet not all happening at once. Yet here she was, focused on me, loving me, asking me if we could be good together. She wanted me!

I burst across the parking lot, running excitedly like I had with Tina at the dog park. All of them laughed, watching me bounce over the terrain as they continued to talk. Finally, I went back over to listen to what they were saying.

Olivia asked, "Come, little one."

She wanted me to walk with her over to the grass. Then she gently picked me up and held me so I was on my back in her arms. Huh? I did not like having my belly exposed! I squirmed, trying to flip back over and be let down. She kept a hold of me though. So I arched my back and leaned up to her face and made a move to lick her mouth. She let me!

"Good dog," she said, then giggled and let me get more comfortable in her arms. Apparently what I did was 'good.' Her energy was calm and loving towards me, but my mind was starting to work; what was she wanting from me? No one had ever held me in such a way.

Next she set me back down on the grass and asked me to play along, in a gentle but knowing way. Then she rolled me slowly onto my back, pinning me in the grass. What? I gave a little snort, again not liking this at all. When I tried to lick her face again, she laughed and let me up.

I did not know what was going on, but clearly she did. Why was she doing this with me? I just wanted to be petted and loved on. But I could see from her face, whatever I was doing was making her very happy. So I played along. Then she asked me to sit while she walked to the opposite end of the grassy area, I started to follow her, when she fell down in the grass. She wasn't moving. Oh, no, what happened? I ran over to her worried and grabbed her sleeve in my teeth pulling gently. Wake up, wake up! Nothing. I tried licking her face. She opened her eyes and giggled and held me close

Wow, I must have done something else right, because her energy grew around me! Okay, now I was having fun! Next she threw a ball, which I chased down and brought back. More praises. This is more like it! They were all cheering when I did that. I liked doing it too, although I could imagine something other than a ball in my mouth—a bird, perhaps?

Then within the greeting excitement, everything slowed down. The woman looked at me with such love, such care. She shared images of loading me into her car and driving away with me. I saw a bed, hugs and kisses, food, and a lawn, other people happy to see me, other dogs and trails that were all to be a part of my life. She wanted me to share this with her. I knew she was thinking these things. I wagged and kissed her. Yes!

As I refocused around me, Elise's smile had a twinge of

sadness mixed in. She knew I wanted to go with Olivia. But I also felt her happiness in knowing someone else could love me and cared to know if I could love them back. Elise was the reason Olivia was here. Their energy was almost identical. Until that moment, I hadn't thought of humans that way, but the energy I felt today carried me to a greater understanding of what Brianna already knew.

Olivia opened the car door; it was clean, not smelly. The front seat held a cozy, soft, clean round bed. It was for me! My very own bed! Elise kissed me over and over and set me in it, the tears welling in her eyes. Austin was right next to her, hugging her, and smiling at me. I knew she'd wanted to keep me. I didn't want to see her sad and almost jumped out to stop her sadness, but she told me I would be 'okay' and motioned to stay where I was. Then she lightly closed the door until it clicked.

Olivia hugged them both and got into the car with me. She petted me with such love, and told me how 'good' I was. I was nervous though. Now I was leaving Elise and Austin, and the last bit of brother too. After watching friends and brother being taken from me, now I was the one leaving the pack. It was different being on this side of the story. I felt such love from Olivia, but also knew the love from Austin and Elise. I watched them wave as the car pulled away. It was another good-bye, but at least now I was going with someone who saw a life with me.

So this was it. This was the human who'd chosen me, and she seemed nice enough to be sure. So far, so good!

The car hum started, and she looked over at me with such love I couldn't stand it and stood close to give her more kisses. As the car went faster, I crawled out of my bed into her lap. She was singing softly to herself; her tone and voice soothed me. She kept petting me as we drove, and I settled in as feelings of calm and safety grew.

We hadn't been driving long when she pulled off the highway and stopped at a building. She found her bag, petted me and kissed me, saying words of great kindness, with an explanatory tone, as she got out of the car.

I let out a soft whine of nervous excitement. Are we here? Is this where I am going to live? But she was just standing outside the car. I watched her every move to be sure she was safe, but she had closed the door behind herself. I couldn't get to her. I began to sing a little—"Hey, let me get to you, so I can be with you."

She went around the back of the car and reached for some white metal boxes with black hoses attached to them. She pulled a long black hose out of the side of the closest box. A light banging noise told me the hose was now somehow touching the car. I cocked my head from side to side, listening and learning the sounds. Olivia pulled the hose away from the car, along with more strange, clunking noises. My eyes hadn't left her. As she got back in, my soft whining transitioned into shrieks of delight. I was close to her again! This was a new feeling, this feeling of wanting to look after a human in such a way, to be with them, to be close.

Once she was back in the car, I looked into Olivia's eyes and rushed to her lap. She held me close, the car started moving, and we were back on the busy road! Rain was hitting the car, and the glass in front of us. Some sticks came out of nowhere, and started moving across the glass. I didn't know what they were and shied away from the sound and movement, but then I realized they were staying outside the car, just moving back and forth, which began to make me sleepy. My eyelids drooped, my head settled onto Olivia's arm, and I could feel her chest moving in and out. It reminded me of my Mama's, and I drifted in and out of sleep, the noises from the car growing distant, lulling me. I felt Mama licking me on the head. I looked up at her and she looked down at me, as I drifted off into sleep.

A few hours later, the car slowed down. The world out the windows looked very different to the one I'd left. There were trees taller than I had ever seen, and rain—so much water coming down, everywhere. It seemed wet like the Highlands of the dreamtime but also awfully bright with lights and busy with cars and people. Even in the dusk, I could feel the hum of busy things. Was this where I was going to live?

We got out of the car. I had never seen so many cars all in one place. The lights, noise, rain, and people were overwhelming. Nothing looked like any homes I'd ever seen, so I didn't think we were home yet. But after a quick pee, Olivia picked me up, and we strode into a brightly lit building. My senses went on overload.

It was so big and bright inside, I began to shake, and shrunk deeper into her arms. I had never seen so many lights or smelled this many smells all at once! Food, dogs, cats and fish? And birds and fabrics, and treats, and other scents that didn't smell natural. The amount of variety and quantity was unfathomable. Were there really this many dogs in the world?

Olivia went down one row, then another, then she stopped in one area. She kept saying the word 'collar.' She was looking for something to place around my neck, something Elise had done also, but Olivia was very excited about finding just the right 'collar' for me. I was excited that she was excited. Soon a leash was attached and I could walk next to her and I began sniffing everything!

We were near lots of dog beds, like the ones at Elise's: all sizes, shapes and colors. Olivia picked out a few, put them in her push basket, and set me on them. I couldn't see out very well so put my paws on the edge of the basket and stood on my hind legs to look out. She laughed and pet my head very softly and said words that made me feel warm inside. She continued to push the cart down each aisle of color, scents and textures. She would lean down and ask me questions, and then put more things into the cart. I realized she was finding things for me. For me! Food and toys went in, until the cart was pretty full, then she rolled over to a narrow space, and a woman started taking things out.

The woman put everything into several bags, put it back in the cart, and we headed back to the car area. Olivia set me down to walk with her. I wanted to run, but my new leash kept me attached. This felt odd, to be held in such a way, but being attached to Olivia wasn't bad at all. The leash let me know where she was, and let me know I was not alone in this big, noisy, bright new world.

On our way towards another brightly lit structure, a family came walking by, with big smiles on their faces and started talking with Olivia. They wanted to pet me, and their touch was loving and kind. I put my paws on them and kissed them. I loved kissing them, and they loved it in return. Then we kept going, and I pulled on my leash towards new scents.

We came across a very short, strange, yellow tree. At least that's what I thought it was. I started asking it questions. Who are you? What are you? I sniffed the air and wove my head back and forth to get a better look. The very short tree did not belong in the world that I knew. I was letting Olivia know something wasn't right here.

She smiled and picked me up. She took me over to the source of my angst and set me down right next to it. It wasn't alive, but smelled like—dog pee! I sniffed all sides and went round and round it several times, to fully assess, and finally squatted near it. There we go; my bladder felt way better. Olivia laughed.

She asked me to sit as we approached a wider space of pavement. I kind of sat but then got up again. I wasn't sure what she meant when she wanted me to sit. Like, for how long, and why? But she praised me anyway and picked me up and carried me towards the door of a shiny glass building. Lots of people were going in and out, and every time the door opened, the smells of food wafted out. I hoped we were going in, and we did!

Inside was full of people, and food, and more people and more food. Olivia went to where the food smells were strongest. She was looking at mound after mound of what smelled like food inside a glass box. My eyes were intently focused after seeing the first mound. I had no idea this much food even existed, let alone all in one place! I became dizzy with desire. Yet Olivia was calm as she chatted with a girl, who put some food into a container. She handed it to Olivia, and I knew it was chicken! Well, Olivia knew what to buy now, didn't she? My nose got more excited, and nudged at the container in her hands. She looked at me and said not to worry, I would get some. At least that's what I hoped she was saying!

Just like the family from outside, humans would look at me smiling, and then talk with Olivia. They would say 'pet' and 'puppy,' and Olivia would say 'yes.' I got to kiss one person after another while they pet me! Wow! So many people wanted to see me and pet me and talk about me and to me. I could really get used to this!

The hunter's wife instantly knew what had happened. They had been admiring the wolf pack for as long as she could remember, and now the moment had arrived where both human and wolf had come up short on their own. Nature and the elements had pushed them both onto the fringe of existence and now, only by helping each other, would either survive.

The wolf pups were the dearest she had seen, and her own children's eyes lit up at seeing them so close and alive, to touch and hold them brought such great joy. For while they would often see them playing in the distance, they had sadly only come across a dead pup now and then.

As they settled in near each other, the mother wolf watched over her pups, being wary at first, but soon realizing the children were like her own. The children's energy was of awe as they touched the fur of the pups for the first time; her pups responded with trust, as they were enjoying the playful energy of the children.

The woman made eye contact with the wolf laying meat near

her, the wolf cautiously took it. More meat was laid out and the pups soon joined her. The children looked on as they all ate together. The food had been shared. Everyone was satisfied. The warmth of the fire felt relieving to the wolf, as her pups began to doze. She too was now more relaxed than she had ever been. Heat such as this had a deep calming effect on her muscles.

Then the hunter stood up, the wolf stood up with him. Their eyes locked for a moment, and he went out from under the pelt into the winter night. The woman was at first alarmed at the stance of the wolf, but then she saw, the wolf was watching her man outside. She sat at the opening of the hut while he relieved himself at the edge of the clearing. She never took her eyes off him. The man, for the first time, felt the eyes of the wolf protecting him, instead of stalking him. He paused as he returned to the hut and realized, she wanted to stay. The woman realized the wolf was protecting them all.

Olivia placed me in the front car seat, then loaded up the food in the back, slammed the hatch shut, and walked around to her door. I, of course, had hopped over to her seat before she got in, eager to see her. She had the container of chicken with her, and as she opened it, she looked at me thoughtfully and said words conveying images of her offering me food. I heard the word 'chicken' several times. Clearly, this was a word she wanted me to know!

As the container opened, I felt an urge to devour the contents, to take it all and eat it all. But I sensed this would not go over too well. Olivia was mothering me right now, and I would never take food from Mama. So I waited, intently staring at the container, envisioning what it would taste like, for just the smell alone was like eating it. She was so impressed with my patience that after her first bite, she handed me one. I respectfully took it from her hand. I got soft pets and big acknowledgment for that, and then she took another bite and gave me one. And so it went until she said 'all gone,' and showed me the inside of the container. Sure enough, there was nothing left.

So, we had eaten our first meal together. The car began to hum and we were back to driving. This time I settled in with a full belly, and a full belly meant everything was all right. She let me back onto her lap, and I fell fast asleep.

As I slipped into my dreams, I found myself once again in the Highlands. This time it was sunny, and the bright green grass and mottled heather was the most vibrant I had seen it. Drops from a recent rain glistened on every surface. The flock was spread out, white forms dotting the landscape, content to be drying in the warmth of the sun, speaking softly to each other of how good and sweet the wet grass tasted in the morning. Brianna sat proudly on an outcrop a ways ahead of me. I trotted to her, at the same time scanning for Mama across the green expanse.

Brianna smiled as I approached, and I gazed into her loving eyes. I shared the deep ancient dream that had preceded my arrival here, and the deep love and mystery of how we had grown together with humans. Her smile grew to a content gaze. I sat next to her, now understanding the world as she did.

At times my eyes would open, and there were more lights and cars. I found it harder to close my eyes, with all the new shapes passing by. Then the hum of the car mixed in with the sounds of other cars around us lulled me back into sleep. I had no idea how long this trip would take or where it would take me, but I felt safe.

The sky was a deep twilight blue, with a streak of light on the horizon. A gentle rain floated onto the glass in front; the sticks rocked back and forth every so often. Out the window, past the lights, the tree shapes looked very tall. It had been a long drive, longer than the one this morning. Eventually, the car slowed as we veered onto a smaller road. I had no idea roads could keep going like this.

Olivia whispered to me, and it sounded like we might be getting close to our destination. For a while longer we drove on a quiet road through rowed fields. It was flat, like where I came from, but as I looked out, I saw large hills rising ahead. The massive trees were so close, it felt like the car would run into them.

Next began a subtle climb up a windy road near some salty smelling water. Olivia was excitedly pointing out her window. The water reminding me of the dreamtime. I knew about Mama's memories of such things, it was the sea. We were by the sea! Were there sheep too?

The road kept winding higher and higher, then we slowed and turned. The lights from the car rocked up and down, lighting the green foliage for moments at a time. We were in a forest. As the car turned along the curved road, the lights swept across the end of the street, more greenery seen, and up an even smaller road we went! It was a slight hill and paved all the way. I began to squeal and whine with excitement; tail wagging.

Olivia's voice was very high also as we pulled up to a house. A house! Maybe this was it! Maybe we had finally arrived! I began to sing along with whatever Olivia was saying, feeling her joy in the air.

I could see the lights from the house windows now. The house itself was tall and very big. The lights grew brighter still as we pulled in front of the garage. I squealed and sang excitedly as the hum of the car ceased. We were here!

Olivia said some words with soft energy, and one was 'girl.' From the way she said it, I understood she was calling me 'girl', and somehow it made me feel closer to her.

I hopped out of the car and into this new world. The smells were: damp, mossy, foresty, musty, rotting leaves, piney and fresh. The piney smell had been subtle when we got out of the car to get the chicken, but here it was full, earthy and fresh. We were definitely in a forest, but with a large expanse of lawn spreading out from the house. The woods must have wrapped around the edge of the lawn, because it was the darkest night I had ever been in.

Olivia let me run around free and sniff. She grabbed a short leash object that she fashioned onto her head. She fumbled around with it for a moment and light began to shine from above her eyes. The light streamed all the way across the yard! She followed me as I went across the grass and had a long pee. I stopped sniffing to take it all in. This area was huge! Wow! If this was where I was going to live, hoorah! All this space, and not one fence to keep me in! Well, the forest scared me a little as I could not see very far into it. Still I ran over to the far edge of the lawn and started running in circles. It was dark, and wet and oh, my goodness, it was cold! I didn't notice how cold until I squatted to pee again, and my pee place touched the cold grass.

Olivia walked me all around a paved area, it was wet but clean. Then we walked around to the side of the house, and then all around the big yard. I felt she wanted me to know where I was, and what it felt like to be here. She was introducing me to where I was going to live!

A small porch led to the front door of the big house. It was open, but covered. I waited for her to open the door, anxious, yet nervous to get inside.

If this was real, if Olivia was really my human, this was where I would be living for the rest of my life. I was excited and scared at the same time to go through the door. What was on the other side? Would I like it? So far, it was nothing like the house I was born in. It was tidy on the outside, more like Tino's home. And I'd liked his home. I liked clean, now that I had been around both clean and dirty. Clean was softer, less noisy, less confusing for my nose. It gave me a sense of peace.

Once the large, wooden door opened, I walked into a small entry room, with a warm tile floor, and a very large collection of shoes. Why would anyone have all these shoes, let alone leave them by the door? How strange—until I saw Olivia take off her shoes and noticed how clean the floor was. There were no outdoor scents coming indoors.

Close to the door, I sized up the series of stairs that led up and away. Olivia saw my confusion. I had never seen this many stairs all in a row and I was glad she carried me up them, as I wasn't sure how I would get up them. Once at the top, the house was open and clean with wood floors. It was warm, and bright, but filled with boxes. Lots of open boxes. Boxes were what Ted had described his family having a lot of before they left him behind.

The boxes made me more than nervous. Ted had been very specific in his description of such boxes. What did these boxes mean? I'd barely arrived, so were 'we' going somewhere? Ted's boxes went somewhere, right? I would have to watch and see if things were going into boxes or coming out.

She pulled out my new water dish, cleaned it, and filled it with fresh water. She encouraged me to 'drink' by pointing at the bowl and gently splashing the water. So I came over and began lapping up the water. After a few drinks I realized I was thirsty, and drank until my belly told me to stop.

When she walked by a box, I noticed her put something in it and start taping it shut. Okay, so these boxes were definitely going. But were we going or was she going without me? My mind started to spin a little.

After she poured some red liquid into a glass, she went

into the bigger room and began piling small pieces of tree into a metal box with a glass door. I had never seen such a thing. But as a flame began to grow, I realized there was something very familiar and comfortable about the light and warmth.

She pulled out one of my new beds and laid it down next to her and asked me over. It was the only soft place to lie on in the room, and I quickly got settled.

She said 'fire,' several times while pointing at the dancing glow. The 'fire' was very relaxing, once it got going, and the heat was soothing after such a very long day. Olivia smiled at me and took me onto her lap. She started talking to me and petting me, and sharing many words. The feeling was kind and inclusive. She had found so many things for me and brought them home, and now she was holding me. I sighed and gave the weight of my head to her arm, letting my eyes softly close. The flickering, familiar light eased my fears and continued to warm my body into a state of bliss.

I wasn't sure how long I'd been asleep, but I awoke to tears falling on my head, Olivia's tears. I felt the sadness seeping from her heart. What was she so sad about?

Olivia's sadness was something I did not understand, but I did understand my own sadness and the sadness of others, such as in Mama and Jade. So who had Olivia lost, and what had hurt her? She shifted and let me crawl out of her arms. I turned right back around and licked the tears from her face. She laughed and cried some more, and petted me, and so I kept licking. She giggled so much the tears stopped, and it was just us together with her heart much lighter than a few moments before. If me giving her kisses and licking her tears away could make her happy, then I felt like I was a part of keeping our pack of two going.

As the mood shifted, she asked, 'hungry?' I had been hearing this word from many people at this point, and it meant food for me! She got up, a little unsteady on her feet, and made her way to another bag brought home with us. She said 'food' and looked me straight in the eye as she filled a bowl.

I excitedly began eating it up. It was tasty, and crunchy, and the first bowl of food I'd ever had all to myself! She poured another glass of the red liquid, and briefly looked at her laptop. She then got up and pulled out food from the humming box that kept the food and put some into a small container and set it on one part of the counter. Within a few moments, food smells began to waft throughout the house, and although my belly was full, her food smelled better.

I laid next to the table as she ate, focused on the food going into her mouth, and what might be in her bowl. I smelled beef. She looked down at me sweetly, and called me a 'beggar.' I wasn't sure what she meant, but I got the feeling it wasn't totally nice, but it wasn't mean either. I studied her face to glean the meaning, to catch an image from her that would explain what she meant.

Hold on, wait a minute! I was not a beggar. This was why we dogs are here, after all, to clean up all the scraps you humans leave behind. Yes, now we live with you, but in the beginning, it was much different. Natural scavengers we were, and we still are. We are just no longer interested in fighting you for the scraps. We started our relationship with you, just out of the light of your fire, waiting, near enough to the kill, waiting for scraps to be thrown our way. We started our relationship over food. You, after all, provided us with all the food we needed and we provided you with protection and hunting prowess and warmth on cold nights to survive. The basis of our companionship is a primal survival love which has grown over millions of years . . . oh, my, where had all that come from?

The knowledge memory flowing through me was very old. I had no idea where it came from, but it was knowledge that felt true. Now I stared at my human in earnest. Did she hear me? Did she understand? Did she know the truth also? She smiled at me. I wasn't sure what she knew, but she seemed willing to understand and kept her eyes on mine. I watched her finish the last bites, and then she offered me her bowl with a few remaining meat scraps. It tasted amazing!

Never had a human included me in her life the way Olivia already had, and we were just getting to know each other! She had pulled me in as much as I wanted to be pulled in. Even in her sadness, she loved me. I felt certain those boxes might be going, but I would definitely be staying.

I hadn't asked to go out, but Olivia seemed to know it was time, and so we went outside.

She said, "Go potty, go potty," over and over and over, and soon I did. I went doodoo next, and she was elated!

Okay, so all I did was go pee and poo, and she got very excited. Well, that was easy enough! Who knew? The cold-damp promptly pushed us back inside. The damp was not something I was used to, so it felt good on my paws to come inside to warm, dry floors.

Olivia carried me to another room. All it had was a bed with puffy blankets and a lamp; another nearly empty room.

She found an extra blanket and placed it on the bed. Then she called for me to 'come.' I joyously jumped up and settled right in. This bed was very soft and cozy. I was getting to sleep with my human on a bed I could jump up on!

With the lights off, it was dark, really dark except for

light in the sky from across the water. No streetlights or city lights were in the forest. I curled into the soft, clean blanket, knowing I was safe. Soon my eyes closed . . .

I was getting thrown out of the truck onto the gravel, where I whimpered and yelped. Austin and Elise waved good-bye; she kissed me on my head. The windows of the car, so many trees passing, the rain. I was running towards the ball and grabbed it. I gave the ball to Olivia. I saw Mama, but then she was gone. I cried out . . . I woke.

I felt a kind hand on me, it was Olivia. She said some gentle words. Her hand was warm and calming. I crawled closer to her and licked her face. I curled into her arm and went back to sleep. I was not alone . . . anymore.

But not a few hours later, I woke up again, this time with a little dribble between my legs. Uh-oh, what was I supposed to do? I hopped down from the bed. Olivia was asleep, but I needed to get out! I let out a little cry, not very loud, just enough to hopefully wake her?

It worked. She stumbled in the darkness towards the door, almost stepped on me twice, but we made it down the stairs to the big wooden door. Once out, I ran as fast as I could to the edge of the lawn. She praised me again for going potty. I never knew I would get praise for something that came so naturally to me.

Back inside Olivia took the light off her head, and I looked up into her eyes; how kind they were. She carried me up to the top of the stairs, kissing my head. I hopped back onto the still warm blanket, and curled in to clean my-self. She settled in next to me and reached over to pet me, first my head, and then my back. The warmth and care in the energy of her hands put me at ease.

Then I heard the words I had longed to hear my whole life but had not known how much I'd longed to hear them until they were said. And when they were said, they were felt deeply inside of my heart and soul. These were not just tones repeated with an action or thing. These words carried a great meaning that I instantly understood.

They were, "I love you."

That night, in the dreamtime, I found myself involved in an exhilarating, fast-moving scene. The sheep were running in one direction and at quite a pace. The terrain was bending and dropping and flattening out. I was in the thick of it, at first not able to find a way out. I used my body to push a space open and found myself on a ledge. The flock was generally moving as one, but a few sheep had been separated from the flock and were trapped on the rocky area.

I ran up to them, speaking in a way I thought they would understand. They stared at me, dumbfounded. I tried again, but they milled in the wrong direction, moving yet farther away from the flock. I was losing my patience. I worked my way around them, and they began to move. I lunged for the one closest to the rear and nipped the area above the hoof. She jumped out of the way but then split off from the other three. Too much. Now she was going in the wrong direction, getting even farther away from the others. I told the others if they hurried they could catch up with the group, and gave a little lunge to reinforce my instructions.

Now it was just me and the lone creature, who had yet to realize being away from the herd would invite an early end to life. She was frightened. So, I calmed myself and eased my way around her. She flinched, but I caught her eye and began to talk with her using my eyes. I kept eye contact and showed her how to get moving. One leg began to move, then the other. One leg then the other; she was figuring it out. After a few short 'keep going' tones, and she was quickly with the other runaways headed back towards the flock.

I woke the next morning, stretched out on the bed with my head lying on one of Olivia's legs. She was breathing softly, still asleep. I had slept very close to her through the night and was in mild disbelief that I was where I was; warm, cozy, fed and loved.

I shifted my position to take in the soft light coming in through the window. The trees outside were even taller than they'd seemed the night before, and they were so green. Everything that wasn't sky was green. I was excited to get out to smell and see it all. I shifted around a little more, and Olivia started to wake up.

She smiled and reached out to pet me. I licked her hands and arms, and she pulled me against her chest and gave me a hug. I licked her face and jumped down from the bed. I wanted to get outside!

But she remained in bed, not wanting to follow me out of the room. What was going on? The day had started, yeah? But maybe not, because she was sad again. I felt it, and she had that look in her eye. I sat attentively for a moment, considering what to do. I decided to lie on the floor next to her bed. I sensed her pain was much like Jade's, a deep pain, but it also reminded me of Mama's, in that she had lost something. Something had happened, and someone very dear was lost to her.

As much as I was feeling this moment with her, I had to pee. So I wasn't going to wait forever! I needed to get her moving and get her to come with me. I licked her face and started to talk a little, reaching out with my paw for emphasis.

"Come on, let's get going!" my energy said.

A small smile began to grow from the edges of her mouth, her eyes lightened. She laughed at me, and I began to wag, still keeping eye contact. She sat up on the bed to follow me out.

The same method I would use on sheep could work on humans too!

Once Olivia was up and out of bed, I immediately ran to the top of the stairs, hoping she would follow me. I really had to go pee; surely she knew this. As I waited for her to catch up, I felt a few dribbles come out—oops, that wasn't supposed to happen. I looked back to her as the droplets hit the floor, and her face was kind, no, understanding. Phew! I didn't know how she would react, but what I did know was potty was for outside only. After all, who wants to step in their own potty all day. Before I knew it, she gently scooped me up, pee and all, and took me outside.

I was so relieved when I made it to the lawn. She watched me go, smiling, and nodding to herself. She was thinking something, but it wasn't about me. There were no words. I wasn't sure what it was, but there was something familiar about it. It was as if she were telling herself to do something differently, in a way, correcting herself. The energy I felt was similar to when Mama had told us to do things differently. But I had never heard a human direct it towards herself.

She said 'sorry,' while looking me in the eye, with her heart soft and open. I went over to kiss her, for now I understood: she was sorry, that is, correcting herself, for not getting out of bed sooner for my potty.

After the kisses and love, I started to survey my new yard. It was huge and grassy and surrounded by the greenest trees I had ever seen. There were small birds chirping and a slight breeze brought in scents from the forest: moss, mushrooms, wet soil, rotting leaves. The smells were pungent and rich, quite the opposite of the yard with Mama and more like the dreamtime. It was a lot to take in, so I sat next to Olivia and looked out and around and up and through. This was to be my home!

I decided to try the obstacle of stairs which prevented me from going from the front door to the rooms above, and from the rooms above to the front door. Surely, I would not be carried up and down my whole life. Up one front paw went, then the other, but what to do with my hind legs? It was a long stretch to get my back leg up there, and it didn't feel right to have all my feet together. I tried to hop up, but I couldn't organize all my paws to stay on the one flat spot and my back legs kept slipping.

Olivia reached out and caught me before my chin whacked the stair. I tried again, and this time she held my backside so it wouldn't slip. In a coordinated effort, my hind paws got up, as I pushed off and put my front paws up. I knew it wasn't pretty, as it felt clumsy, but with a little help, I made my way to the first landing. I was so excited and wiggling I almost fell backwards, but Olivia was there to keep me on track. So up the next set we went, and the last try was almost graceful!

Once at the top, Olivia went into the food place and was singing as she made my breakfast. Now we were working together! My bowl was filled with food again, and I ate until I was full.

She fixed her own 'breakfast', and after, started moving the boxes to the top of the stairs. The boxes were filling up with all of the contents of the house. Eventually all that was left was a carpet, a big screen, and a table with some seats for her to sit on. The boxes were then closed and taken down the stairs, one after the other.

On one of her trips down, I heard a knock on the door. I called out "Hey, who is that?" Olivia was down there! I had to get to her, to protect her from whoever was at the door! I rushed to the stairs and took the first one, but the momentum from running pushed me too far over; the stairs were coming at me too fast! I tumbled onto the landing in a heap. Olivia was right below me and cried out some words of concern, but I was more worried about her than me. She said some words of encouragement, and I tried the next batch of stairs. This time I was more successful, still calling out the whole time, "Who is that at the door?!"

The 'who' at the door was a woman of immense stature. I could see her through the entry window next to the front door. She was smiling from ear to ear at the sight of me. I began singing with delight; someone was happy to see me, and Olivia was happy to see them! I quit feeling worried and was eager to meet this new smiling person.

Once the door opened a crack, I was out fast and ran past her legs, then came back to dance around her. We all went out to the lawn, where there was more room for me to do my sprints and drive-by hugs. I ran like a crazy girl around and around, until the woman bent down to pet me and let me kiss her. She said soft words I had never heard before and was quite enamored with me and my squeals. She and Olivia were laughing and sharing words and looking at me with big smiles.

At one point the woman gave Olivia a hug, and I felt a wave of sadness come over her. I sat and looked up at her, and then to the woman, then back to Olivia, recognizing the sadness she had been feeling last night and this morning.

We all came inside and the boxes began to get carried out, accompanied by laughing, loud banter, and some more tears. The shifting energy made me nervous. With all the boxes leaving, I sought reassurance by pawing Olivia's legs and looking up at her. She gladly obliged and hugged and kissed me. 'Kaye', as I heard her called, gave me sweet hugs and pets too.

"You are staying, and we love you," the hugs said.

As the morning changed to afternoon, all the boxes had been carried out and any noises I made echoed in the empty rooms. Kaye left by way of the backyard forest as she must have lived somewhere beyond the trees. Olivia was using something stinky on the boxes when a very large vehicle pulled up in the driveway. I gave the usual warning. This time the human visitors were men, who pulled a long ramp out of the back of the truck and began loading in the boxes.

Olivia began cleaning up inside. She used a loud, rolling noise machine—that thing was scary, and I ran to the far side of the room. Olivia noticed right away and made it stop. She picked me up and walked over to the windows to watch the last of the boxes were loaded. The loud door shut. The sadness in her grew again as the truck headed down the long driveway. I watched it go, nestled in Olivia's loving arms.

The house felt very empty, and it must have been a bit much for Olivia, because she began crying in earnest. She slumped onto the floor and put her head in her hands. The room by stairs filled with the scent of sadness. I sat in front of her and waited for her to look up. I wasn't sure what to do. What would she want? She kept sobbing, until the tears ran between her fingers. I put my front paws on her leg and began to lick the tears from her hands.

She lifted her head and looked into my eyes. I began licking the salty tears from her cheeks. She gave a light chuckle and a deep sniffle, and picked me up to hold me closer. I would not stop licking her cheeks, and she just kept holding me and laughing softly, until she began to smile at me. She said some soft, kind words, and the word 'love' again, which I instantly felt in my own heart. The energy began to shift. It felt like a storm clearing. The moment became softer, calmer, and her breathing returned to normal.

She kissed me on the head and gently set me on the floor. She began chirping some lighter words, and a smile began to brighten her face. I sensed maybe something fun might happen! So, of course, I followed her down the hall. I hadn't been to this part of the house before, but we were in a space with a lot of clothes. She took off the ones she had on and pulled out different ones; I smelled each piece of clothing as she put it on. She began to say the word 'walk' over and over. She was asking me something. I searched her face to see what it meant; her tone told me this walk thing had something to do with me!

Sure enough, she went back towards the front door and grabbed my collar and leash. I was so wiggly, she had a hard time getting my collar on. She asked me to 'sit,' which I was able to do for a moment, but then I got up again. She said it again, this time a little more seriously and looked me in the eye. I sat longer, and she was quick to get my collar on. Then she clicked on the leash, put on her shoes, and we were ready to go!

Getting outside into the fresh air made me feel great. The sun was shining, the leaves were turning color, and we were walking in my very own yard! We made our way down the paved path, and in the distance was shimmering water. The view was similar to the dreamtime: blue-toned water in the distance, darker and lighter hues rippling and delivering a salty scent. It was great to be walking with my Olivia and exploring the area, although we passed by a place where a sad-looking dog was locked in a cage, softly barking at us. This was the source of the barking I would hear! She was pacing and moving in a way that didn't make sense to me. I'd heard of such a thing from Ted but hadn't seen it for myself. I wondered where the dog's human was.

As we continued along the road, I ran from one side of the road to the other, as far as the leash would stretch. There were so many scents to follow—rabbit, mouse, cat, dog, deer and, oh my, a coyote?

The scent of coyote gave me pause. It was old scent, at least. I flashed back to the one I'd met and had no desire to ever meet again. At least I knew now to be on the lookout around here and was glad Olivia was with me.

We came upon other houses along the street, spaced farther apart than back in Elise's neighborhood, and surrounded by trees. The trees were abundant, and so tall. Very tall! We kept walking until we crossed another road, and then up a narrow dirt path full of tree roots and leaves that led to another wider path. That path went right through the forest. This was turning out to be excellent fun.

The scents of other dogs mingled along the edges of the forest trail. All kinds of leaves I had never seen before, filled the area around me, highlighted by patches of bright green moss, like the dreamtime, but also fallen branches, and more types of trees, rotting logs and funny-looking mushrooms. Some of the leaves were tall, at least half as tall as Olivia, rising up from the ground in dense clumps. Each leaf had many smaller leaves that I soon realized were very fun to run through.

I smelled many, many dogs on this path. Just today I'd smelled at least as many as I had toes for. Some were old, some young, there were none my age, and one had something wrong with his heart. I knew how many boys and how many girls. None of them smelled like brother or Mama, but I didn't think they would be this far from home.

The trees went on as far as I could see, and we were in the midst of them. I felt very small, in some ways much smaller than I had back in the open fields, because I was now in the presence of these giant structures that shaded the ground and were so close together it was like being in another world. The air was different in the forest world, cleaner and somehow fuller. Not being able to see very far through the mass of trunks and ferns pushed my sense of smell to be on alert for other critters.

We veered onto a smaller path and started up a slightly uphill path going deeper into this forest world. The ground was springy and mostly covered in leaves and needles from the trees, but in places the roots were so big we had to jump over them.

I heard Olivia give a big exhale. She was getting calmer the further we went. Walking uphill was not something I had done before, and I found myself panting very quickly, as if I had been running, but I hadn't. We went a ways further, and Olivia said it was time to turn around.

Going downhill was much easier, and she released my leash so I could run with full enthusiasm! I bounded down the path, pushing off the shallow banks and dancing in between the leafy clumps, only to turn right around and rush back to Olivia. I'd run right past her and then flip around and run past her again. It felt like the dreamtime; experiencing true freedom, the outdoors, and my own nature flowing through me. This was more like it!

And what was also more like it, was Olivia. She was humming, giggling at my craziness, and simply being in the stillness of the forest. The forest 'air' was shifting her energy to calm but with a tinge of joy. I was happy to see her mood lighten and happy to be sharing my zeal for life with her.

Over the next half-moon cycle, the nights seemed longer for Olivia than for me. She would have the fragrant drink at night by the fire, cry a little as we watched the sunset, and then we would go to bed.

But I was still learning to hold my potty overnight, and so at least once, but usually twice, I would wake her up during the night to go out. I know it was hard for her to wake up in the middle of the night, but she never refused me. Once awake she was all about my potty, and how 'good' I was, which led to lots of pets and kisses as we settled back on the bed.

After a few nights, she was pretty tired during the day, and so it wasn't uncommon for her to doze after dinner. Aside from that, over the next few days, I was able to get Olivia on a schedule that worked for both of us. I'd wake up first and lick her face to get her out of bed with me. We'd go outside, I'd potty, come back upstairs, and she would feed me. Since she was at home in front of a screen, I had my bed by her desk, and would keep myself occupied with various toys and some trips outside with her to run and practice bringing things back to her. In addition, she also took time to love on me whenever she got up. This included kisses on my head and my muzzle, belly rubs and sweet talking love words. She was so very affectionate with me, it made my back toes curl with anticipation.

She spent a lot of time at that desk. So when late-afternoon came for our longer walk, I was beyond ready, and I knew she was too. After our walk in the trail filled forest, she would shower in the shower room, and I would protect her while she showered, by laying between her and the door. But this time, I got a little bored, so I started to wander down the hall to a place I had wanted to explore since I first arrived—the area with all the shoes.

To be honest, the shoe scents had been calling to me so strongly that walking past them every day had become unbearable. My curiosity was innocent enough; I took a pass over every single shoe in the room and came across one that had a slight food smell. I gave it a quick lick; only a drop of food, but I found it was an interesting texture, this shoe! I tested it further with a tentative chew. It was soft yet hard, not anything like my toys upstairs. When I chewed a little harder, it felt really good. So I chewed again, and it felt even better. Finally I began chewing in earnest.

I was so very consumed with this pleasure I didn't notice Olivia standing not a few body lengths away from me. The look on her face was one I hadn't seen yet; it was not happy.

In fact, it was a look of shock and dismay, followed by a flash of anger that went right through her eyes and into mine. Uh-oh. I could feel many different emotions flowing and swirling around her, but what came out of her mouth was "No!"

I let the shoe fall out of my mouth. My head lowered and my tail tucked. I backed away from the shoe, as she grabbed it. From what I saw, the shoe I'd chewed looked very different now from when I started. She threw the chewed-up shoe down, and stomped past me up the stairs. I heard her yelling, which made me shrink a little lower. Then she came back downstairs.

"No!" she said again, and pointed to all the shoes, which she then began to pick up and put away in a box. One pair was left out, but she put them up high on a cabinet. She did all this without one word to me, and very little eye contact.

The last human who even vaguely acted like this was the man who threw us out of the car. Was Olivia going to throw me out of the car? When she sat on the stairs and asked me over, I stayed put. I wasn't yet sure of her intentions; she was a human, after all. But my eyes stayed on hers, and I felt the chaos inside her head. I sent her my love with all my strength.

"You love me. You told me so. I felt it, and know it deep inside. This is not the true you, this is the chewed-shoe you. I am sorry I chewed your shoe, I didn't know."

I then sat, perfect form, just the way Mama had taught me; ears fly way out, legs tight underneath, chin held high, but not too high, and lovingly stared into Olivia's eyes. Her eyes began to soften, then tear up.

I came closer to her, wagging in "acknowledgment." She gently picked me up and held me close while we sat on the stairs. She looked lovingly back at me through her tears, and I stayed with her gaze. She said "sorry," and I could feel her heart slow even more. She said other kind words, words of understanding. And I understood the images in her mind. She had picked up the chewed shoe and shrugged her shoulders, while saying a word of correction to herself. She was explaining it all to me. She said the important words again—'I love you'—and this time the words pulled us into a moment where we were sharing the same feeling, and there was nothing more to explain.

The feeling that began to fill the space was one of unity. I was no longer a dog, and she was no longer a human. We were one connected flow of energy; inseparable and coalesced. Our understanding intermingled: her life flowed into mine, and my life flowed into hers.

A deeper commitment was taking place. This was not the dreamtime; it was our time. I saw her running and driving and working and having tears, arguments, and laughter and kissing. She saw me with the coyote, saw my Mama's eyes, saw my brother leave, the man throwing me from the truck. Our lives were blending, and as they swirled together, a deeper love swept through us both. A new life was being created that moment. The path forward was revealed, full of light, love, and joy. We ran together, learned together, slept together, cried together, healed together, found new friends, had car rides, shared food, went swimming and ran on the beach. She and I were now a real pack.

When we went out to potty and take in the energy of the evening, the sunset was softened by gathering gray clouds. By the time we headed in, a light breeze brought with it the scent of rain. She talked on the phone as we flowed into the evening routine of being snuggled up by the fire, and watching the fading light through the large windows that looked out over the water. Tonight was the first time she hadn't shed any tears while holding me. My heart felt her heart opening to my love.

As the fire waned, she looked at me with a question in her eyes, then soft words followed. She was asking me a question. But I was unable to feel or see the meaning when she said the word "Schatzi." She seemed to like that word, because she said it a few times, "Schatzi." Our eyes remained in each other's gaze, as I wished I knew what she meant.

Eventually we settled into bed, and as she held me close,

she said "Schatzi" again, kissed me on the head, and drifted into a peaceful sleep. I watched over her with a deepened sense of responsibility. There was now a connection, a soft light between us, that removed all doubt about my belonging. I had crossed into a familiar place, the place once occupied by the feelings of comfort Mama had provided. Olivia would never leave me, and I would never leave Olivia. We had become a pack today. We had bonded. My love, my ancient love, had reached her, and she accepted being a part of my life on a deeper level, one based on safety and mutual understanding.

I contemplated what my role in this new pack should be. Olivia provided me with food, shelter, great affection and love. What would I give? I felt a desire to protect her, but could I? I had a great ability to run and to scent, so I could stay aware of our surroundings, and let her know what was around, or who was around. I was joyous, gave great kisses and love, and loved to get her to smile. I was loyal and humble; surely these traits were valuable. I was off to a great start!

But Olivia had strong feelings, and there were things I could do that were not pleasing to her. I wanted to know what was pleasing and what wasn't. How would I learn this? I certainly didn't want to repeat what happened with the shoes, not if I could avoid it.

To my surprise, the familiar but long-absent glow of Brianna entered the room. I thought Olivia might wake, but her breathing didn't change as the great wolf and I regarded each other.

"Love has many roles, the pack requires many roles. The pack is love," Brianna said.

How was it she knew exactly what I was thinking? Before I could ask, she was gone, but I sensed she was proud of me. I had many things to learn, but I was on my way to living out the Code.

A few days later, a car came up the paved path towards the house. I raced down the stairs to look out the entry window with Olivia right behind me, saying words of excitement. She opened the door to let me run out and see who it was. A woman was getting out of the car, and I greeted her warmly with wags and squeals.

"Hey, who are you?" was my greeting, mixed with "I can tell Olivia knows you." The scent of many dogs wafted from the car.

"Hi!" said the tall woman, with long, wild, blonde hair. Her complexion was lighter than Olivia's, and her eyes were bright green. I was very excited as she reached down to pet me and I put my front legs up on hers to get more information. She began talking with me immediately. Her tones were higher and more engaging than Olivia's. I found myself drawn to the energy behind her words. She knew how to communicate with me better than Olivia did, but why was she here? Olivia chatted with her, and it was very relaxed between all of us.

I wagged my tail hard, hitting one of her legs over and over. Who was this new person? I really liked her! How did she know how to communicate with me so well? Her heart was big for me, and she had just met me.

Inside she took off her coat and promptly produced a bag of treats. As we walked up the stairs, she let me sample a few. They were new and savory. She walked around the middle part of the food place, the new snacks held in her hand low enough so I could reach them with my mouth. She kept walking around and around, with me close by her side, licking up the new snacks from her hand. Each time I took one into my mouth, I heard a click, and happy words from her. I wasn't sure where the clicking was coming from, but I was liking this! I was getting treats and feeling the love.

Around we went, around and around and around, until I was getting a little dizzy. The woman noticed, and we started walking in the other direction. The newness of the activity left me panting with excitement. So we rested for a bit. I laid down at their feet, as the words 'good' and 'Schatzi' were said over and over to me.

I realized I was the topic of the conversation because they kept looking at me and saying the 'Schatzi' word. Olivia gave me a big smile and grabbed the treat bag and started doing what the blonde woman had done. As she looked down at me with love in her eyes, I understood. I was Schatzi to her. That is what she called me. That was her name for me.

The blonde woman—her name was Cynthia, like mine was now Schatzi—would come over periodically. The visits with her were my favorite. Cynthia had a way about her that was different from Olivia, but to be sure, Olivia was learning that way too.

What I had learned, was if I did something and heard a click at the same time, then it was something I was supposed to do, as the treat came right away. It went like this: I did something, Olivia would click, I would get a treat. Which progressed to: I did something, Olivia would say a word over and over while I did that thing, and I would get a treat. Cynthia was showing Olivia how to communicate with me, and we were learning so many new words together. Walk–sit–stay–lie down–stand–bed–down. These were words I was learning, and I was learning quickly!

Her cues were solid and consistent. She really wanted to communicate with me, and I was more than eager to learn.

It became simple: what to do, what not to do, and in many cases it was more like remembering than learning.

I was very gentle in general, but there were some things I did that were not okay for our pack. For example, I liked exploring the world with my mouth, and these days my gums were a little sore, so chewing things made my mouth feel better. I liked mouthing people's hands, tasting what they had on them, but the soft bite part was not what Olivia wanted me to do. Jumping up on people who came around me was something else not to do.

Then there was my impulse to nip ankles and lower legs while people walked or were running around outside or even walking up the stairs. My instinct said they were sheep if they were moving that close to me. Olivia and Cynthia understood the motivations for my behavior by the way they appreciated my skill, they knew it was just me, but regardless, it was painful to them when I nipped their legs. But these were the skills I came with; having aligned with the Border Collie side of me, it was my nature to herd sheep and tell them who was in charge—but the people were not sheep. I had to 'unlearn' in this case, which was more of a challenge, as it went against my deeper nature.

When I nipped I was gently told 'no' and they added a little 'yelp' also to show me it hurt. I realized 'no' was reserved for the serious offenses, the biting and nipping. Otherwise, to curb my jumping, they taught me 'off,' and in a half moon cycle the new tones and words also had meaning to me. I was learning to communicate with Olivia!

In the days and weeks that followed, Olivia and I found something which brought us both great joy: and that was training. I was excited to wake up every morning and see what we were going to learn that day, or what we would practice, or what I could show her I knew. It was all a part of getting to know each other better, and she was ready to join me.

Olivia was telling me the words she wanted me to know, and I was learning them in an effort to work with her as a pack and, of course, I wanted to please my human! The excitement of learning a few words made me realize that I could learn more. I came to know things easily—quick in speed and in mind. Any doubts in my heart as to the type of dog Mama had produced were fading away. Why, I was everything any human would ever want in a dog!

Olivia's bouts of crying were lessening and her smile was becoming a regular part of our days now. It seemed our growing love was beginning to heal her heart. Olivia saw there was still a life to be lived around her. In much the same way Mama had given brother and me a lot of extra attention after my sisters were taken away, Olivia was giving her extra attention to me. When I lost Mama, Jade had been there for me. Now Olivia and I were here for each other. It was turning out that I had found a human who was even more attentive and affectionate with me than Jessica.

Olivia was learning, and fed me out of her hands now most of the time. Maybe one meal a day was given in the bowl, but every other meal was given from Olivia's hands. She was learning that the way to my primal heart was through my stomach. I felt the loving energy when she fed me, and moment by moment, our bond deepened. The energy of her hands was kind and generous, offering me the nutrition to keep me growing and strong.

She understood the importance of the moment that started it all; survival—companionship through food. Food had bonded our kind to humans from the very beginning. The first moment Brianna's pups took food from the woman's hands was the very moment that changed the course of our kind forever. Trust, love and nurturance were discovered on another level when shared with humans. We found humans could follow the Code of the pack when they so desired.

One night, as I drifted into the dreamtime, I was especially hoping to see Brianna. I wanted to ask her my first question about Olivia. I emerged into the grassy green glow and soft mists and was welcomed by the flock. Most were lying down but others had spread out to graze up higher near a heather-covered slope. Brianna was on the slope, watching over all of them.

I quietly made my way toward her, so as not to startle any of the sheep. Brianna and I walked along the ridge line. I shared about Olivia letting me love her and was happy at times, but I also sensed she still held onto a sadness. I wasn't able to fully put together who had left her life, but I did know the effect it had on her.

Brianna had shared many images with me before, but this time it was quite different. Still in the dreamtime, she took me beyond the realm of the Highlands to another realm all together. We emerged in a forest clearing. Beyond the frost-covered branches of the trees, I saw smoke rising from a fire in the distance. It was cold, and my paw pads felt numb. Brianna's gaze held mine for a moment, and she asked me to follow her quietly. As we crept closer to the source of the smoke, I could see it was a camp, with many people, mostly women and children. Their houses were made of tree branches covered in animal hides. There were dogs too, but they looked more like Brianna than like me, smaller, but not at all like the scary coyote. Their manner was calm and proud.

Out from one of the tree-branch houses came a woman. She looked strong, yet her expression was somehow both clear and troubled, yet loving towards the dog that lovingly followed her.

"The woman is Rajyna, and she lost her mate to the winter," Brianna explained. "Her dog is Kiala, my great, great granddaughter. Kiala is now Rajyna's other half. That is her new role in this pack. Kiala adored Rajyna's man, Lannar. He was good and kind and loved Kiala like his own, but he fell through the ice and never got warm again. Part of Rajyna's heart died with him, and until she can re-grow it, Kiala will be the protector of her heart. That is her duty now, and she gladly accepts it, as she too misses Lannar and wants to be strong now, for all the strength he gave."

I began to understand as Brianna said, "You are Kiala to Olivia. You are the protector of her heart until she can re-grow it. You have found a good human if she can love you even while she is in so much pain."

One morning after breakfast a familiar "Hello!" came from the woods behind the house. It was Kaye, the neighbor who'd helped Olivia with the boxes. She had already become a regular visitor to our scene. I gave a quick announcement, then the song of familiar joy: "Hey, someone I know is in our yard!"

"Who is that, girl?" Olivia would respond.

I looked at her intently, having learned the association between those words and someone we knew arriving at the house, then bolted down the stairs for the door. Sure enough, it was Kaye, but today she had a black puppy with her!

"Omg, omg, omg, omg," was the equivalent of my loud squeal. "Open the door, Olivia! Open it! Open it! Open it!"

She cracked open the door, and I burst out. I didn't know who to say hi to first, Kaye or the puppy? It was a girl, kind of shy, and she pulled back a little as I rushed to her and started licking her face.

"I am friendly. Let's go play!"

That was all I was about!

She looked different from my brothers and sisters. She had wavy charcoal-black hair, and a thin, funny tail that curled up. She had long legs and was much thinner than I was. Her heart was shy, but she was a puppy! She looked at me with kind eyes; she would never hurt me, ever, which got me even more excited. I ran over to the grass, and she shyly followed me. Next I rushed toward her but flew fast by her.

She turned her head to nip at me in play—"hey, slow down."

I looked back at her—"try and catch me!"

I loved the game of chase, mostly with my brother, and there'd been the fun moment with Tina at the park, but here was a chance to do it all over again. I kept running as fast and silly as I could, and soon she started after me.

"Go, Chelsea!" I heard Kaye yell.

After many, many rounds of chasing, fake biting, and wrestling, Chelsea and I both collapsed on the shady side of the lawn, our tongues lolling out on the cool grass. It felt so good. I rolled a few times to feel the cool all over, then rested on my elbows with my belly in the grass. Chelsea was lying on her side, panting with a smile, looking over at Kaye and Olivia. They were chatting and laughing. What a great morning. I wanted to do this every morning.

And so it was! It became the routine that Chelsea and

Kaye would come over after my breakfast; our mamas would have coffee and look out over the yard. Chelsea and I would play and play until we were both spent. She was my best dog friend in the whole world. She was my new sister.

By the passing of another moon, Olivia and I had learned enough to bring me along in the car to her world outside of the house.

I was meeting all kinds of new people everywhere we went. People were always happy to see me, so it was very fun for me to jump in the car and go places I never had been. I would wiggle and wag and walk all at the same time towards these new people. Most of them loved this, as it showed how excited I was to meet them. But we had to work on the jumping and the mouthing, because I really liked getting close to people. I wanted to lick their faces and mouths, the way Mama used to lick mine and I would lick hers, but since they were standing up I had to jump to try and get closer. It was hard to control my exuberance, but eventually I learned to stay down: people who wanted to be kissed would crouch down to see me. Olivia would beam with joy.

Morning playtime with Chelsea and Kaye and daily walks were now part of the routine at the house. Olivia worked around these activities, and she didn't seem to mind spending more time outside earlier in the day than later. I was steadily learning new words, and being on the trail let me test some of them out, but mainly our outside time was about having a good time and for Olivia to get out and walk and talk with Kaye.

Today though, we went further along on the trail than ever before. As we crossed the bigger road and picked up the trail into the forest on the other side, the smell of salty water grew much stronger. The trail went across several streams that Chelsea and I of course had to run through, splashing and dancing as we went. Then the trail narrowed, and the smell of things rotting with a salty aroma grew and grew. My senses were awakening to something I hadn't yet experienced but felt excited to see.

We followed the zig-zagging trail down a steep rock face, and soon we were hopping over two metal rails with strange, hard rocks around them that smelled oily. But once across, the narrow, softer trail continued, and through the trees, what I started to realize, was water shimmering below. Chelsea and I started to run as fast as we could towards it and soon were in a full sprint to see what was just beyond the edge of the forest.

Past a rocky outcrop, the ground became soft and white, with many old, worn logs, and a very salty smell. The water touched the edge and we flew into it before realizing it was so cold! My senses went on overload. The texture of the sand on my toes, the coldness of the water, shocking my legs and belly, the scent of decaying seaweeds, small animals, bird poop and other yummy scents all mixed into one big sensory meal.

I learned right then, Chelsea was a water dog! As in she felt at home in the water. Just like I was good at telling the sheep where to go and when, she was good at swimming and doing things in the water. Seeing her wade right in and immediately swim was so amazing! We were both dogs, but we had different skills. For a moment, I wondered how it was possible, but then I got caught up in trying to follow her and ended up with a mouthful of cold water.

She told me to keep my legs moving like I was running. I tried it! One leg, then the other began to move from the sand under my feet, and my head stayed above the water for a few moments before I scrambled back to the shallows. My first swimming attempt wasn't at all graceful, but Olivia and

Kaye cheered me on anyway.

Once out of the water we splashed and ran and rolled in dead and smelly things. The texture of the sand, soft and shifting, made running a physical feat, as it was hard in some areas, soft in others, rocky then wet. Strange and new scents changed with every step. It was by far the most fun I'd had in my life, and I was doing it with my dear sister friend and my Olivia close by.

A moon cycle later, Olivia had brought a large box-like structure near her desk. It was made of fabric with see-through material on all sides. It also had a top that was able to be open. One of my soft beds went in as well as some of my toys. I looked in after it was set up; very curious. The sun was coming in through the top, making it warm inside the box.

The new box sat for several days, and then one afternoon Olivia crawled in, so I followed her. She curled up on the soft bed smiling. We stayed for a little while, and she petted me and snuggled me and gave me treats. The next day, she put my food in, with the zipper door open so I could eat by just putting my head inside. That was fine enough.

She kept calling it a 'crate.' Once in while, she would put a treat in there. I would go in to eat it quickly, and then leave. This went on for the next several days. She said, 'crate this' and 'crate that.' Olivia and I would go in together, and which I liked. One day she encouraged me to get in the crate all the way and then motioned for me to stay.

She sat right outside and petted me through the door. After a few moments, she let me out. Well, that wasn't as great, but at least it was short. Other times I would just crawl in to sleep, and before I knew it, my time spent in the crate was increasing. I wasn't quite sure of the purpose or why Olivia didn't want me near her all the time.

Sometimes I'd be in the crate and need to pee. I'd whine a little, and she would let me out promptly. I realized the time I spent inside was increasing a little each time. Then she left me in the crate when she left the house. The top was open, and I had plenty of light and toys and a few treats which took me a while to work through. She wasn't gone long, so I was relieved at that. But what I realized was although I had to go pee, I had to wait until she came back, unless I wanted to foul my own bed.

She was very consistent about letting me out when I was staying in the crate. When she let me out, it was a joyous reunion with a lot of praise and love. Apparently, I was doing something right by hanging out in this confined, yet friendly space. As this 'training' went on, I found I could hold my pee for just under half a day. That was as long as Olivia would ever leave me. She was usually with me, but grew to understand I couldn't go everywhere with her, and I wasn't quite ready to roam free in the house unattended.

Eventually, it came down to having me stay in the crate at night. I protested with a soft cry. Olivia wasn't happy about it either, and she would come and soothe me and then go back to her bed. One night she came out with her pillow and blanket and slept next to my crate. I wasn't clear about why this even had to happen, but she kept using the word 'training,' and I had to admit, I could now hold my pee longer than ever.

A few nights later she asked me into the crate but left the flap open while she went to the bedroom and left the door open. I wasn't sure what to do. Did she forget to close the it? Was I supposed to 'stay' regardless? I waited as long as I could stand it, and then very slowly and softly walked into her room. Her light was on and she sat up to see me come in.

My low-wagging tail communicated, "Should I be fully happy you saw me? Should I be here?"

She smiled and patted the bed. I raced and jumped up next to her. She held my head close and looked deeply into my eyes kissing my nose and cheeks and top of my head. I was back in my rightful place, on the bed next to her, between her and the door. That night I held my pee until morning!

It was hard to believe so much had happened during the cycle of a few moons as I was learning so much. But what I was about to learn next was one of the most important concepts of all: 'come.' The concept, as I understood it, was a little different than just knowing when Olivia called my name.

She'd say "Schatzi," to get my attention. But after that, what was I to do? The next word was what gave me direction: 'Come.' Come meant 'go to Olivia.' This was easier said than done. If I was close by her, coming to her was easy enough. But if I was farther away in the house, or busy doing something more interesting, I would just keep on doing it. What she was wanting was for me to come to her under all circumstances.

Today we found ourselves outside, learning how to come to Olivia in the yard. Now, the outside was a very different setting than the house. First of all, the house was a very predictable and structured environment. I knew where everything was and all of the sounds; it was not a living structure.

Outside was ever changing, stimulating in sound and scent and my senses came fully alive; I was my truest self outside. Part of who I was, was a dog who could hear and follow commands from their human at any distance. That's what my Mama did, and her mama before her. And Olivia wanted me to not only hear, but respond to her regardless of circumstance or distance. In the house we had progressed from coming a few body lengths to coming from one side of the room to the other, to one part of the house to the other, to just hearing the word, and not seeing Olivia, to downstairs and upstairs.

Cynthia was a very enthusiastic part of teaching me to 'come' outside, as it took more than one person. I would start at a few body lengths away from her. Then Olivia would say 'come,' and I would run to her, and she would click right as I arrived and give me a treat. Then Cynthia would call to me, and I would run to her, repeating the process. Gradually they made the distance greater between them, so I had to run farther to get the treat. I stayed focused on the treat, and soon I realized I was running from one side of the yard to the next. I was doing it!

My ability to work with Olivia this way was growing a connection between us that I didn't yet fully understand. I felt great freedom of not having a leash on outdoors, and sensed she was feeling the trust that I would come to her when she wanted. It reminded me of moving with the pack, feeling each other's moves and needs, never a desire to be far away. I wasn't sure if that same connection was possible with a human, but by learning Olivia's words and intentions it was beginning to feel that way.

At least a few times a week, I would go over to Kaye's house to visit with Chelsea, especially if it was raining or stormy out. Kaye had so many more toys than Olivia, and toys were allowed to stay all over the house, and not always put back into a basket after play. The random nature of coming across them during our sessions of chase made playing in the house even more exciting. She also had a big area of floor which was carpeted, and two high areas with soft cushions we could jump on! This meant we could run around as fast as we could, then jump up on the cushions, jump from one to the other one, then run around again. It was the same fun as chasing Chelsea in the yard, but brought inside and with more obstacles added to the fun.

As Chelsea and I got a little out of breath or too hot, we would take a break. We'd get a drink and happily chew on some amazing treats Kaye would offer us: pigs' ears, some yummy crunchies she made herself, tough beef chews, braided beef, or pork skins. Then we'd pick up the chase again, or just lie around in post-play, full-tummy bliss.

Most days it was really hard to go back to Olivia's. Not because I didn't love her, I just loved to play more and be with my dear new sister, Chelsea. Sitting around, watching Olivia work at her desk didn't occupy my mind enough, and I would become restless. Even though she loved on me often, it wasn't the same. It didn't take long for her to notice my reluctance to come back home, and I could sense a twinge of sadness in her each time she came to fetch me.

On one of our walks, Olivia took us back to the small trail she first showed me, only that time we'd turned around. But this time we kept going. Up, up, up we went. I was growing bigger and stronger and more agile. I felt the excitement of going further and walking somewhere new. New scents, new sites, deeper and higher into the forest we went.

I showed Olivia a wide grin of excitement and thanks, and she looked at me with the same feeling. We were outside together. Nothing, not even playtime at Kaye's house, made me happier than being out with her in the wilds, feeling so alive, feeling the pack.

We kept going until the trail went different ways. She chose the way going up a small rise. I sensed the direction of the sun, it was taking us towards the water. Soon we came to a clearing overlooking the trees that swept me away! The sky was part sun, part clouds, but we were looking over forest now. I could even see a road down below, not to mention water and patches of trees in all directions. We were higher in the hills than I had ever been. It reminded me of the Highlands and gave me a sense of place, of peace and joy.

Olivia crouched down and offered me water from a tube that went to her mouth from a pack on her back. Somehow a stream of water came out as she placed it over her hands. I drank eagerly, getting about half of the water, as my tongue sloshed the rest of it out of her hand, but she kept the stream going until I was full. I thanked her with a wet lick-kiss on her mouth. She wiped it off, and smiled. As she looked out over the land, I felt her happiness being here with me. We were able to share this moment, and become a little closer.

She stood, looking around, saying some words that felt very kind, but she wasn't saying them to me, she was saying them to the moment, and to our surroundings. My curious nose kept me sniffing about, which led to leaving a few pee messages for those who would come next.

My full-on exuberance going up the trail left me a little tired as we started back, but going downhill was much easier, and I flew down with very little effort. Olivia joined me, and we flew down the trail together. As we ran, our energies combined. Running together in this way was very familiar to me, with our glow at its brightest. We were the essence of Kiala and Rajyna.

Whether we drove out to have fun in the car or walked out to get to the trail, we had to pass the caged dog's house. She was alone in her cage most of the time, howling and wailing a good part of each day. She would look out with great sadness, and other times be curled up with her back to the road.

Sometimes she would call to us: "Why am I in here? Please let me out." Or it would be almost a whine: "Why won't you let me out of here? I'm so cold."

To experience one of my dog sisters in a cage all day, was deeply disturbing. Why was she in a cage? Why wasn't she with her human? Dogs were not meant to be in cages, I knew no animal was. I was free and having some of the best moments of my life with my Olivia, while this dog was suffering daily with her human. The contrast made me sad and confused.

It confused Olivia too, who spoke unhappy words under

her breath about the situation whenever we passed by. I felt her sadness, and desire to do something about it, but also her frustration about it not changing.

I was living the Code that Brianna and Mama had taught me, that the life of a dog held great value to humans. Our bond had been forged in the great fire of survival; we were integral to humans' lives. My human treated me with re-spect, and honor. She was learning as much about me as I was about her. She brought me into her life and included me; she wanted a pack with me. She was living the Code. I'd now experienced this truth firsthand.

But what had this dog done to find herself in such a place? From what I was learning so far: nothing. She had done nothing to deserve a life in a cage. She was simply not with the right human. Not all humans followed the Code.

On one of those windy, rainy, Highland-like days, during a car trip around town, we pulled into an area with a lot of green trees with branches like the ones in the forest. But these trees were not much taller than Olivia, and all lined up. Happy tones were playing and lights were twinkling, and many people were dragging these trees and putting them on top of their cars. What?

Olivia let me out with my leash on, and we began to walk around the rows of the trees also. The fresh tree aroma was overpowering. It was so concentrated my senses became light and happy. We walked around several trees and back to another one, and then back to the first one, and she finally pulled one out. A man came to help her, and after some fussing, we too had a tree on the top of our car. But not before Olivia quickly laid a blanket on the car itself, to make a nice bed for it.

This tree business had my curiosity going. What were

we going to do with this tree? I could think of one thing, but why did we need to bring another tree all the way home for that when we lived right by some good ones?

Once home, Olivia dragged the tree right into the house. Up the stairs she went, all the way to the top, finally setting it down in the main room. She then jogged back down the stairs, and I followed her, thinking it was a game. After rummaging in the under-stair place, she produced a strange-looking plastic bowl with straight pieces attached to it. It also smelled like a tree. So this had something to do with the tree. I tried to carry it in my mouth for her, but it was too awkward.

I was beyond curious at this point, and watched as she lifted the tree and set the bottom of it into the bowl. How strange? She then started turning some knobs on all of the straight pieces, and soon the tree was standing up straight, well almost. She stood back, tilted her head one way then the next, which reminded me of me. Then she did some more twisting and turning, and the tree was a little more straight. Finally, she stood back and gave a quick nod. She was happy with it.

Next she poured some water into the tree's bowl. Then it was time for her red fragrant liquid, and then she got out some boxes, several to be exact, and what she pulled out of the boxes made me very happy indeed. Toys! In the boxes were tiny toys of all colors and textures. Of course, I had to put them in my mouth, and while she was looking in one box, I gently took one from another box and put it next to her on the carpet. I wasn't into chewing it; I just 'wanted' it.

It was gray and red, with two eyes and a very big nose, and was made of a fabric that felt really good in my mouth, but mostly I just wanted to be part of the fun and have my own toy.

She pulled out some thin, leash-type strings and poked an end into the wall. All of a sudden, tiny lights came on. Little lights, all along the strings. She wrapped the glowing leashes around the tree—they were like the little sun sparkles on the water at the beach. Except they were inside the house, hanging on a tree!

She went to her laptop, and soon tones filled the room. The tones were happy and cheerful and she began to sway and move to the them. I knew what she was doing, and I loved to join in. Together we were both prancing around the large, near empty room, with our tree, our tones and our lights. She put another toy on a branch. Then she pranced some more, took another sip, and repeated the process. This time, I knew what she was about to do, so I went to the box and pulled out a toy and brought it to her.

Her face lit up as bright as I had seen it, and she laughed with such joy, and hugged my head and rubbed my ears and gave me kisses on my nose and cheek. 'Good dog!' and 'amazing' were her two favorite words when I did something really great. And here they were both used at the same time. She let me set the toy in her hand, after she asked, then she put it on a branch. I went for another and another and another. This was fun! After many trips, the tree was full. All the toys were on the tree, except for the first one I had pulled out on my own. She asked me some questions about it, and I tilted my head to understand. Then I brought it to her and she placed it low on the tree, at my eye level. I realized she had put all the soft toys where I could reach them. She loved me.

A few nights later the wind started to pick up until it was forcefully thrashing through the trees. The next morning we woke to no lights in the house and branches scattered everywhere outside, covered by a thin layer of white ice. The clouds were a deep gray that said more was to come. Thankfully, Olivia didn't need to go anywhere, and so our morning potty doubled as a reconnoiter of the damage. We surveyed the scene, even down to the paved road where the last houses lived. I heard buzzing machine noises echoing through the forest from all directions.

She looked at the branches, then she asked me a question. I sensed it was a question for herself, but by the way she looked at me, somehow I was involved.

She started to pick up the thick branches. I instinctively grabbed the end of one and pulled. She spoke to me and used the word 'play,' which meant 'did I want to have fun?' But I tugged the branch out of her hand and began to carry it towards home. No, I wanted to work. Which earned a couple 'wows' and 'amazing,' on top of her wide eyed grin, as she knew I was helping her. But I knew how to work, and if she wanted this wood for the fire, I was ready to help out!

Until long after our potty, I helped her clear and haul branches up the paved path to the tree branch house. I was herding wood for the fire! It wasn't sheep, but it was putting things in their place, and I was doing it with Olivia.

Back inside, Olivia started a fire, made me breakfast, took a bath, and with the lights back on, settled back at her desk for the remainder of her work day. I sat by the window, watching the clouds change shape and move, and soon become white.

Every moment added a little more of the mystical white cold stuff to our yard. By afternoon potty break, I was able to sink my nose in it and sniff the mice burrowing into the flattened grass. I would snort, then jump, then run, and spill and roll. It was amazing to feel this crazy substance—it got my juices running.

"Snow, Schatzi, snow, snow, snow." Olivia repeated.

Another new word. Snow. This was snow! The yard had transformed before my eyes. Tree branches had turned into smooth, white forms now bent under the weight of white. It was quiet and still, more still than I had ever experienced. What few birds were around were keeping to themselves. The sky was a patchwork of various gray shapes, lit from below by the all-white landscape. It was another new world. Some smells were muted by the cover of snow. And they would rise back as my paws kicked the cold snow away. The crisp air was so exhilarating I forgot about the growing lack of sensation in my paw pads. When we walked out to the trail, I could barely recognize it. It was all white and puffy with a few branches popping out here and there. The urge to run as fast as I could through the soft substance overcame me. So I did!

The full purpose of the inside tree with lights was revealed to me one afternoon when some brown boxes
arrived. Olivia opened the brown boxes; and brightly colored packages were inside. As she placed them all under the
tree, I sniffed each one, assessing the contents and potential
owner. None of the scents were familiar to me.

That night she brought out more boxes, and paper, and
items from bags, and the same cheerful tones filled the room
as she began to wrap the items in colorful paper. One after
the other, she placed them on the colorful blanket under the
tree. I was curious about one of the smaller ones, so while
she was busy wrapping another one, I laid down with it and
found an edge with my teeth to start tearing it open. The
sound of the paper tearing turned Olivia's head. At first she
had a startled look on her face, but when I looked up at her
with big eyes of innocence combined with play, she smiled
and went back to her wrapping.

The next day, Olivia started to clean up the already clean house, and was cooking more than usual. She was on the phone a lot, and our routine was shortened to a quick walk on the trail.

Just as she got out of the shower, I heard a car come up the driveway and announced. When I ran to the door, a woman with bright clothing, holding several bags was grinning at me through the glass. Feeling the friendly vibe, I began to sing.

Olivia, barely dressed, hurried to greet our guest. Joyous voices and words were exchanged between them, along with a long hug, laughter, and an introduction to me. I saw by Olivia's behavior this human was part of her pack, so I continued to sing with happiness at the possibilities of getting to know her better. My enthusiasm was immediately reciprocated. She got down to my level, hugged me and let me kiss her face all over.

I hadn't seen Olivia this happy with anyone. They continued chatting as we went upstairs, and soon opened a bottle of drink, settling by the fire. There was laughter as the woman looked around the bare room. At least Olivia had lots of pillows to sit on.

Not much later, more cars came up the paved path. I announced with great excitement, running down the stairs. Olivia opened the door and let me run out and meet them all! The arms of our new guests were loaded up with packages and boxes of food, and large black boxes which made noise as they were pulled along behind them. Those black bags had been places!

I had never been around this many people, except for the time at the dog park with Austin, and here they were all coming to our home. Laughter and hugs and more glasses of drink were passed around. I was jumping up and wagging and so excited, I grabbed some toys to bring into the fray. I figured this was going to be fun, and I wanted to play too!

As more packages were placed under the tree, I sniffed each one, sensing some of them were for me. Soon everybody moved to the food place, and the smells of all kinds of food began to fill the house. One woman was putting plates on the table, another was making something with green leaves and another was making drinks. The energy was light and loving and kind. It was good to see Olivia with people with such caring energy. I saw the glow connecting all of them, and I was in that glow.

Once they finished eating, they all moved to the next room to be near the fire as Olivia and I went out for a quick potty. We joined everyone on the thick, soft rug, while they all grabbed pillows and got settled around an open bottle of the red liquid. The chatting softened into quieter tones. After getting some soft kisses and gentle pets, I stretched out in the middle. It was simply bliss to fall asleep surrounded by the love and laughter and warmth of such humans. The room may have been empty of things to sit on, but tonight it was very full of love.

The rainy night became a rainy morning, and I was so very anxious to get going, as we never had people sleep over. I wanted to check on everyone and see how they were doing. Even during sleep, my senses had been aware of their presence in the house; more pack for me to protect. So as soon as Olivia was awake, she understood my exuberance and let me out of our bedroom. I excitedly ran downstairs to fetch them and was greeted with shrieks of delight. After some pets and love and all-around greetings, the smells of breakfast began to waft down the stairs, and I was eager to get everyone back upstairs to eat.

The conversation grew as we watched Olivia put the biggest chicken I had ever seen into the place that heated the food. I was very, very, very excited, knowing Olivia would share parts of the chicken with me. As breakfast was finished, they all drank some more coffee and sat around the tree. I was finally going to find out what this tree with all its packages was all about.

Amidst laughter and smiles all around, Olivia offered me the first package. She prompted me to 'take it'—the words she used for anything she wanted me to take in my mouth—so I did. Whatever was inside the wrapping was soft.

"Open it, girl," Olivia offered, the same words she'd used the other night while I ripped open some of the packages she had just wrapped. There was no formal training around it, but I put it together that this 'present' was for me, and I was about to find out what was inside. I went to work on the paper, gently tearing away small pieces at a time. Everyone was enthralled and giggling at my skill and progress. When I looked at Olivia, she was beaming with pride.

My 'present' was a soft, furry toy with both squeaky and crinkly parts. It was very colorful and felt good in my mouth. By afternoon, I had opened all of my presents and some of Olivia's too. The scent of big chicken had filled the house, giving me visions of the meat Olivia would share with me. So I headed to the food place to wait by the warming place until it was ready to come out.

Once the big chicken was out of the warming place and on the counter, my mouth began to water. My imagination overtook my stomach, based on the bits of chicken Olivia had given me in the past. The big chicken didn't smell exactly like a chicken, but it was close enough. My eyes stayed focused on the bird. While plates were set out, more and more types of food were served and finally, when Olivia cut into it, drops of my hunger were hitting the floor.

She kept cutting on the bird and placing pieces on a big plate; scented steam rose into the air with each cut. Every so often, she would drop a few little pieces on the floor for me. Then she cut a bigger piece which she fed to me by hand, it was very fatty with skin. My eyes rolled back with pleasure.

They all sat down at the table, and I laid down on my nearby bed, intently watching them eat what I knew tasted amazing. I didn't have to wait too long before the plates were set down for me to 'clean.' Potatoes, gravy, bits of the chicken that wasn't quite chicken, some leaves, and cranberries were left on each one!

The mingling of flavors sent my tummy into ecstasy. I kept licking and licking until the dishes had no smell of food left on them. Everyone laughed at my commitment to leaving no morsel behind. The big chicken was then cut into many parts, some put into a big pot, others into a large container, and some into my food bowl. I was getting fuller by the moment, and feeling satisfied.

The rainy weather had stopped for a while and let some sun peek through the fast-moving clouds. Olivia's friends put on clothes to go outside, and out we went into the forest path. It felt so good to feel the air and take in the scents outside after being inside so much the last several days. As we walked along the trail, other people and their dogs were walking around in a similar content state, and I smelled the big chicken on many of them.

After the walk, we settled around the fire and felt the day wind down. As the conversation and laughter carried on around me, I stretched out again on the rug, letting the warmth and my stuffed belly lull me into a deep rest. I was so happy to be around Olivia's people for this many days. I could see where not having them around would be sad for her, just as me not having brother or Mama around made it sad for me.

Long after it was dark, I felt her gently place me on the bed, and she drifted into sleep herself. The day had been full of food and love and laughter, and it brought us both great peace through the night.

A half moon after her people had left, Olivia pulled out the tree boxes and began to pack away the tiny toys and lights and other colorful shapes. The inside tree had been with us for a moon cycle and provided a comforting presence as the days of darker clouds and heavier rains ran together. A few days after it was gone, I found myself more into napping and less interested in going outside. Sure, I still gave a soft announce when certain trucks or people would go by on the street, but in general I was mellow.

Storm after storm would roll in, and Olivia would wait for a break in the rain to take me potty or to go out for a short walk. I had grown so much and was feeling all of my body working together. I zoomed up and down the stairs that had once seemed so hard to climb, and my ability to learn kept increasing.

Night after night was spent by the fire. Olivia would spend time looking at her screen or an object made up entirely of paper, I would play with a toy or work on a dried beef ligament and eventually, I would settle next to her until bedtime. We slept together, woke together, took rides in the car and shared times with friends, both indoors and out. I was never more than a few body lengths from her at all times. We shared a combined field of energy.

The newness of these life activities grew familiar; I was learning all the elements that would make up my day. Wake up, potty, breakfast, play with Chelsea and say hi to Kaye, walk, lie around or play with toys while Olivia worked, learn some words throughout the day, walk again, eat, potty, watch the sunset, sleep, maybe a potty in the night, sleep then wake, and have it all start again, and of course Olivia would love on me every chance she could.

But something stirred in me as I began to learn all these elements; a desire to have them happen in a way that made sense, to me. I was starting to see the day lay out in a pattern and a pace, how everything Olivia and I did, connected to the next thing we did in a certain way. And as I made these connections, I began to herd Olivia to stay with it. The main points were when I was to be fed, or walked.

But this realization spread into smaller elements that made up my day also. I now had an opinion on what I wanted, not a strong one mind you, but one where I realized a preference for how I wanted my life with Olivia to look.

A great example was Olivia had lots of socks, and when she took them off, she tossed them in a basket for her already worn clothes; sometimes a sock missed the basket.

When that happened, I would collect the sock in my mouth and take it back upstairs to my main bed. By the end of the week, I would have quite the sock collection around my bed. Olivia would giggle and smile when she gathered them up and take them to the room where the humming machine took the clothes.

When it came to putting my soft imitation animals away, it took some gentle cueing on my part to get her to realize that she was living with a dog, not a human. Although I liked collecting her socks, I also liked having some my things out and about, not all put back into my toy basket. This was an aspect of Kaye's house that I really liked and wanted to have in my home also. It took many, many moons for Olivia to leave my toys lying where I'd dropped them, but once she did, I realized she had accepted an aspect of my style of living.

But there were times she would go around and collect all, of my toys, and put them back in the basket; and a little later, people would come over. Soon I realized if she was picking up my toys, and the rest of the house for that matter, people were coming to visit, so that made it okay.

We had worked on the distance 'come' over the whole dark season, and now I was pretty good at coming from quite a ways away outside. This made Olivia very happy, and made me proud to feel her trust.

She usually had me on a leash when we went on the trail, but there were times and places where she didn't use it. If she was on her rolling thing that let her move without feet on the ground, or running a part of a trail that was narrow and rocky, these were situations where she wanted me to learn some ways to 'work' with her, off-leash.

The dreamtime had taught me how to move to make the sheep go where I wanted. Now Olivia and Cynthia wanted me to move certain ways when out on the trail. My training was a progression. First I learned how to be 'down,' when I was near Olivia. Then she would ask me to be 'down' a body length away, this added to my prior knowledge. And now, as we neared the season of the high sun, she wanted me to be 'down' whenever she said the word, no matter where I was.

If I would be a ways ahead of her on the trail while running or she was on her rolling thing, I would hear 'down' and look back to her waving me to the side. It took me a few moments to put it all together, but then I got it. The idea was to stay 'down' until she came to me. This was then reinforced more by her going past me, and waiting for her to 'release' me. Which, when it happened, was joyous and encouraged with treats and love. I learned these commands and responses easily, as they were akin to how I already moved in the dreamtime with my own flocks! We were now moving as a pack through the forest!

On a warm night, out in our grassy yard, we were playing with the soft flying floating thing that I would
then catch in my mouth. Olivia called it 'Frisbee'. Shelly,
the neighbor dog from the cage, had made her way into our
yard. Sometimes she would come over to potty when she
was able to get out. She had such a humble nature, but this
time she was more submissive than I had ever seen her. Her
head was lower, and she didn't want to look me in the eye.
I felt her spirit was deeply wounded, and she was doing the
best she could to keep going day after day in the cage.

I stopped playing to say hello as I had been wanting to
ask her how she was surviving her life, such as it was. Her
answer was simple, yet complicated. She told me she loved
her human.

"I am living the Code, just as you," she said.

"But how? How can you love her, even though she ne-
glects you?"

"Because dogs love humans; it's who we are. And no, my human is not living the Code."

Her words gave me pause. She was right, we did. We did love humans. We were the Code. But Shelly had not found a Maria, although she had tried. Shelly told me she'd escaped to my yard several times before I'd arrived, hoping that Olivia would take her in. I desperately wanted to help. I looked to Olivia—surely, we could help?

Olivia understood the plea in my eyes and her answering look expressed that if she had taken Shelly, her human would have just come over and asked for her back. The images went on, showing Kaye and Olivia talking with a person in a uniform, him shaking his head, pointing at Shelly's cage and getting back in his truck and driving away. Even Olivia had spoken to, and ultimately yelled in frustration at Shelly's human on more than one occasion, only to be met with a blank expression and the door closing in her face; and nothing changing around how Shelly was cared for.

So, Shelly was to be left with that human and took comfort from any contact she had with nice humans and friendly dogs. The man who brought the packages became her best human friend. And although her moments of joy were few, she was always grateful when they happened. I realized, her story, could have been my story.

My body was now full grown. I'd shed my puppy teeth many many moons ago, and along with losing them found myself not wanting to listen to Olivia. I started asking why to her requests or commands. I also started to sneak away when I could and help myself to the big neighbor dog's food. It was tasty. After a few weeks, Olivia noticed I had gained some weight rather quickly. That, and mites had infected my muzzle again.

The first time I got mites was a few moons after coming to live with Olivia. She gave me all kinds of different foods to get them to leave me alone, and finally after several rounds of changing what I ate, she found some food that helped the mites go away. It also had me feeling much better. The food was oil from salmon, raw lamb in little dry wafers, and green granules that smelled like the ocean. Sometimes she would just give me raw meat, and sometimes raw bones. She began to mix it up as these were all smells and tastes I loved, and had me feeling great right away! But something I was eating now was making me not feel great.

So, after one of our hikes, she confronted me with the questions. Why was I getting heavy? Why were my mites coming back? She looked at me discerningly, probing for answers. I meekly looked back at her, soft eyes, staring up at her. No answers found.

The next day, while she was cleaning out her car, I started to do my usual 'I'll sniff near the bushes and drift out of view, then race as hard and quietly as I can over to the big neighbor dog's food bowl.' It was overflowing with food and covered in flies, and I started to gulp it up, like I hadn't eaten for days. This time the bushes rustled behind me, and Olivia emerged, eyes on fire.

"Schatzi!" she scolded.

Olivia marched towards me with big energy. I hastily swallowed another gulp before I slunk away from the bowl.

She quickly sized up the situation. Here was a huge food bowl for the huge dog that lived next door, with his day's worth of food. His day's worth, was many day's worth of food for me. Not to mention the bowl was moldy and foul from the combination of drool and food waste commingling for months on end. Olivia shot me another stricken look. I stared back. It was found food, and it tasted good. End of story.

She shooed me back home, muttering to herself. She said so many words I couldn't keep track, but few of them were loving. I had grown to know her yammering was just her way of expressing how she felt. But when she turned away from me and went inside, I stared after her, knowing that she was very disappointed in me. Probably the worst feeling I could feel was to disappoint Olivia. Here I was, stuck between my primal self and my love for my Olivia. My primal self still had control of several aspects of my life, and acquiring food was one of them, but living with a human was teaching me other ways to live. I knew she loved me, and all would be okay once she finished saying her unhappy words. What I didn't know was I wasn't getting any dinner that night.

Short trips in the car were pretty common these days. But when Olivia started to unload everything from the car, and pack bags and items from her desk into the car, I knew something bigger was going on. I started to lie by the open bags, saying, 'You are packing me also, right?' She would smile and walk over to me and say kind words and kiss me. At that point I began following her everywhere through the house.

As we went to the car, it was getting pretty full. On the next trip out, my main bed was set in place in the backseat. It looked cozy, I jumped in to assess; not bad. I could see out the front window while lying down, and it was very soft. She asked me kind questions, to know if I liked it. I jumped out and wagged. 'Yes, this works!'

Everything had a place. It was all very efficient, down to where my food was kept and access to my water bowl. Once on the road, I was seeing things I had never seen before.

The world we drove through was much bigger than the world of my day-to-day life. So many buildings, and cars, and trees, and hills, and distant mountains, and water; it was all so new and stimulating.

Eventually, we would get off the busy road, and we'd pull up to a building. Olivia would crack the car windows, run in, then run out and come to get me out. I would pee a little, she would give me a yummy, water, and food for a few minutes, then ask me to 'load em up,' and click me into my seat belt. Then she would drive to a line of cars, slowly move to a window by the same building she had gone into earlier, and a nice person, with nice words, would give her a cup through the window. There would be a pile of yummy cream on the top that she would let me lick. Then we would go to the place with the hoses that went in the car. After a few moments and a 'click,' we were back on the road! The whole stop would last less than one of her showers! That became our road routine.

We would go for long stretches between stops and every stop was a new world with new scents and new people. One place would be hot and sunny, then another would be cold, depending on the time of day and where we stopped.

We would stop for the night at big buildings with big beds. I was amazed at how tired I would be after not doing anything in the day, except lying around in the car. But Olivia seemed just as tired as me! So once settled, we would fall asleep almost instantly, then wake up really early the next day, and do the same routine again!

After a few sunsets of driving and staying places, we arrived to an area with many buildings and cars and I was overwhelmed by the size of the roads and how many cars were on them. Whew! Olivia was driving faster and more jarringly than I had ever experienced, yet there was an ease in the way she moved our car among the other cars. But this much movement made me anxious. So I braced myself as best I could against the backseat as she shared assuring energy and words to calm me. They conveyed, 'It's all good, and be patient.'

We finally descended into a wide open area; Olivia kept saying, 'the Valley, the Valley.' We went around winding turns, up and down hills on the big road and turned onto another, only to line up behind a herd of cars where we almost came to a stop. The cars were slowly crawling towards the sun as it drifted lower in the sky.

Eventually the herd began to move faster, and we pulled

off the road and parked in the shade at what looked like a food place. I knew it was a food place by the color of the bags people were carrying in and out. It was cool in our car, but when Olivia opened her door, hot air rushed in. She quickly closed the door, beeped me in and hurriedly walked towards the store. I took in the new scene and waited.

Waiting in the car was easy because Olivia never left me for very long, and I was entertained by the people going by. Each human's energy was quite different from the next, so it kept my attention. Some were old and tired, others in a hurry and stressed, still others were giggling and laughing. It was quite the mix. Plus Olivia always gave me a 'treat' when she got back, so that was something to look forward to. Sure enough, it wasn't long and she was rushing back to the car with a full bag of food.

She handed me a 'treat,' as expected, and said, "Such a good girl!" I had learned that being patient and waiting was something Olivia greatly appreciated about me.

Then she pulled out a can of bright green yummy sweet water I had seen before and was drinking it fast. She saw me eying it and poured some in my car bowl. I drank it all: delicious.

Once buckled in, we turned onto a very busy street, then onto another with many large trees. One thing I noticed about this new place it was the amount of cars living here. More than I had ever seen. Yet here we were, in a neighborhood that felt like home. The trees by the road were big and the houses nicely kept.

Olivia was driving pretty fast up a steep, windy road

and once we got to the top, opened the window in the roof. The dry air flowing in was full of new scents.

We then began a smooth descent down the road into a canyon filled with trees. We turned sharply onto a smaller road and slowed. She opened the windows behind her and the smells of the canyon began to fully flow through the car. My head was resting on the sill, feeling the air blow through my ears and nose. We were surrounded by green and yellow trees and shrubs. It was dry, dry, dry, like where I was born. My nose was picking up all kinds of scents: frogs, rabbits, coyotes, bobcats, dogs, cats, horses, goats, chickens, sage, mesquite, and dust, lots of dust.

The air cooled quickly as we dipped down around a bend and passed over a stream, the damp scent was instantly calming; so many frogs were singing! We wound around again, up another smaller, winding road. By the time we turned sharply into a narrow paved car path and pulled in next to a house, I was singing my 'wow, are we here?!' excitement song, knowing we had made it to our destination.

I heard joyous calls from a dog and a woman as we got out of the car. Olivia said 'Hayley' several times. This woman's name was, Hayley—waved from the patio deck above us, and a big black dog named Spot came and introduced himself. He was strong, vocal, and kind.

As Hayley made her way down the stairs from the upper deck, Olivia grabbed my bowls and bed and brought them inside. Whenever she did this, I knew we were staying for a while. She filled my water bowl and set it near my food bowl. I took a long drink, as she and Hayley continued to bring in our things.

The space inside was very tall, clean, and bright, but the walls were not far away. Fresh flowers were on the counter, but there was no place to sit except for a desk. I was used to Olivia's empty-space habit, but I didn't even see a bed for us to share. Where was the bed?

I sniffed around the floor thoroughly, taking in the

information of who was here before us. It smelled okay. Above me, I noticed steep stairs, that I could not conceive of climbing up. They led to a place that Olivia kept referring to as a 'loft.' She saw me sniffing up those stairs, and I was tentatively pawing the lowest step, working out how to get up them. She paused for a moment. Clearly she had not thought about how I would be getting up this obstacle. But in the end she picked me up, and carried me up to the top. The bed was up there! In addition, this high vantage point allowed me to see the entire space below, including the door. I had only enjoyed such perspective in the dreamtime, when I would sit atop a rocky outcrop and watch the sheep below. To sleep in such a confident position, would be very comforting indeed!

After the bed question was solved, she carried me back down, and we got settled into the new tall, but very small space. Olivia was chatting, Hayley was helping, Spot was wagging. It felt good to be here. As I watched Olivia unpack, I was hopeful. We were in a new place, with nice people, maybe her sadness didn't follow her here.

The air was dry and warm enough to leave the windows open, day and night. The night sounds in the 'canyon' were similar to where I was born, but magnified. I so enjoyed the sense of sleeping outside, but knowing I was safe inside. The chirping cricket song filled the night, but was frequently interrupted by the shrieks and banter from the local coyotes. Sometimes it was so loud, they must have been right by the house. I was alarmed, but we were inside, up high and safe.

Within a half moon cycle at our new home, Olivia started to be away for long periods of time and that made me sad. Olivia was my companion now; we did everything together. I felt she wasn't happy about being away this much either. Every time she left, she would hug me and convey our life would not always be like this. Her leaving especially made no sense to me, as she used the word 'work.' Why would she 'work' away from home? And if she was sad, and

I could feel it, then why did she go?

Olivia understood, and knew I would not tolerate being home alone by myself, I was too people oriented. So to alleviate some of the sadness of being apart, she invited someone to entertain me a good part of the day. The human visitor Olivia invited was 'Rachael,' and she was lighthearted and a dog lover. It wasn't my first choice to share time with Rachael, but she was very caring and we had fun.

One of the mornings before Olivia left for work, she pulled a large object out of a box. She pulled it apart, and began to put food in it. Then she put it back together. This was new. I sniffed it. I saw her put the food in, but now I could not see it. But I knew it was in there. This fascinated me! She opened it again, and a few of my special treats and yummies went in there also.

It was during my next nap, the object with the hidden food began to buzz, then move. I tilted my head to one side then the other, to better understand what was happening. As I watched, saw some of the hidden food came into view. Amazing! The fresh scent confirmed what I saw. I hopped down from the couch and sure enough! It was a treat! I ate readily, and waited to see if it would move again. It didn't. I used my paw to 'encourage' some movement. But nothing happened. After a while I grew bored and crawled back on the couch. But later, as I was looking out the window around 'lunch' time, the object buzzed again, and this time my lunch came into view. And so it went until dinner was served. From then on, I would watch Olivia load the feeder every morning. I knew she wanted to feed me herself, but showing me that food was prepared gave me a sense of calm throughout the day. I knew my belly would be filled.

The time Olivia spent away from me, left me to think on what my life would be like without her, as I missed her so much. What if she had not been looking for me and brought me home? What if I had ended up with someone like Ted's humans? Or worse; Shelly's?

During the stretches of time that Rachael wasn't with me, I would drift into the dreamtime, and run with Brianna as much as I could. Her company was good for my soul. She reminded me of the fullness of life, and her company kept me from missing Olivia too much. Of course it also helped when Olivia would come home missing me as much as I had missed her. We would have a joyous reunion every time! I would bring her a sock, kiss her, and she would get down on the floor with me and hug and kiss me, letting me know just how much I meant to her.

One morning, Olivia began loading my things into the car. I began to dance and sing. She was taking me with her! I was wagging, wiggling and singing. And as she bent down to pick up my leash, I licked her face all over to emphasize: 'this makes me oh so happy!'

We drove fast down the winding road through the tree-lined, rocky walled canyon. Back and forth, side to side, cars flashed by Olivia's window. I was happy when we reached the bottom of this road, as it wasn't as curvy by that point, and the landscape flattened out and became more open. A salty scent came through strong; I could smell the ocean! Soon we popped out right out in front of the biggest swath of blue water I had ever seen. It went on into the sky.

From here, our trip heading into the sun was just as fast but not as curvy. The beach sky was wide and blue. Olivia rolled the windows down on the water side of the car. I rested my head on the door ledge, in awe at how the big water seemed to flow into the sky. I watched the waves crashing and felt the sea air wrap around my nose. How full and varied the scent of the seaweed was: dead, but alive, savory and salty, all at the same time. I knew seaweed from our forest home, on the beach where I'd first tried swimming, but here it was more fragrant. There were blooming flowers, and different trees. Even the sand smelled lighter. It was so much warmer here, like the days of long light back home.

Olivia let out a 'whoop' as we sped through a curved tunnel and emerged onto another big busy road. It felt like the car was flying—until we would suddenly slow down and she yelled some angry words. I knew those words were not for me, but I felt them anyway, and tucked my tail.

"Aww, baby," she said, looking at me in the rear-view mirror. She stayed pretty quiet after that.

Not long after, we were at 'work.' Work was a pretty big place. The ceilings were as tall as a house, but open, with a lot of wood. The floor was like stone, but smooth and shiny. Inside was a collection of odd-sized and shaped rooms. Some of the rooms were open, some closed, and some were dark and others were lighted, but all of them had people looking at glowing screens. Just like Olivia!

Olivia took me to meet a thin woman, with long blonde hair, who was very excited to see me! She must have been a friend of Olivia's. I wagged and hugged and let her know, how glad I was to be with them all!

I went with Olivia to work many times after that exciting first day. Olivia's days were long, long, long, starting before dawn and ending deep into the night. Being inside all day wasn't my favorite thing. But at least I was here with my Olivia, and all day people stopped by to pet me and feed me and adore me.

One day, while we were in the big screen room, the guy who told Olivia and other people things throughout the day, asked me sit on the chair next to him. Up onto the chair I went, and he petted me while talking with every-one.

This room was very dark. Images played over and over, then images would pause and they would point and talk, and they would play again. Olivia and others would point to the screen and talk and sometimes nod.

"Schatzi?" the man looked at me and began asking me a question while pointing at the big screen. Every one was laughing. I guess he was asking me something that was fun-ny. Or maybe I was somehow being included in the 'work' they were doing here. I looked at back him, not fully un-derstanding, but feeling how he was including me. I wasn't sure how to respond, so I kissed him. Everyone laughed again, and he said kind words.

The best aspect of work, outside of being with Olivia, was the food. There was always a lot of it, and people shared with me continuously. But as much as I loved the food, I could not see coming here forever. And when Olivia would sit back in her chair, long after our bedtime and look over at me with tired eyes, I sensed she felt the same way.

We lived in a canyon full of trees, and animals. It had a wild, natural feel to it. After being around the cars and big buildings, I was happy to come home to the feeling of wild nature. Olivia like being here also. The canyon was healing her spirit; it was getting lighter each day we were here.

Our 'out in nature' time came up on the 'ridge' above our canyon home, usually before or after work. The ridge was exposed to the wind and sun, and was wide open to the blue sky.

Blue skies were pretty common in the land of dry air. As beautiful and open as the ridge was, I soon learned it was a place where dogs could run free, without leashes. This was exciting to me, as I could run free, but knew how to 'come' to Olivia. Most of the time, the dogs were well behaved, but most didn't know how to 'come' to their people. Others wanted to try and fight me, for whatever reason. It took a few times of this happening for Olivia to begin to protect me, and also begin talking to their people.

Olivia would become worried when the dogs were coming towards us without a clear intention as they were a good distance from their owners, who clearly had no control of them.

I would often hear the owners say the word 'friendly' in these situations, which most of the time was not the case. The dogs who would run over to us and push their way into my space were not friendly. They were pushy and domineering, wanting to assert some type of control over me or have me bow to their will, neither of which I was interested in. It made me tense and I would snap at them to leave me alone. Olivia would then have to maneuver around the pushy dogs to avoid the negative interaction. On a few occasions the dogs were actually friendly and it was a pleasant exchange, but that didn't happen very often. I learned to keep my distance and just focus on getting by them.

Outside of those chance encounters, we had fun, and learned the less popular times to go, to have the ridge to ourselves. Some thing I very much looked forward to seeing were small, mouse-like creatures that dug all kinds of holes and would pop their heads out every so often. I was fascinated by them, and would stalk and watch them for as long as Olivia had the patience to wait for me. Sometimes we saw rattlesnakes—like the kind Mama had once run into. One time I even nosed one, but it was too sleepy to respond. That time Olivia stayed calm and asked me to come, so I did. We would see a different one almost every day; initially they scared Olivia to her core, but soon we got a sense about them, and just gave them a lot of room.

As the days grew hotter, the sun on the ridge would heat my black fur more quickly. And although I enjoyed the open feel and soft breezes of the ridge, it was getting uncomfortable to be out for any length of time. I longed for the cooler temperatures of our forest home and shaded trails. Olivia could sense my discomfort, and as soon as her work was done, we took the long drive back to our bigger home.

I had been with Olivia for a second season of the leaves dropping, and the nights had been getting colder. The fire was going every night, and we would cozy up on the couch until bedtime. Our walks and runs were mostly in the rain now, and I would wear a jacket, which kept me dry but not clear of mud.

Once home, she would hose me down outside. The first time she washed me off, I had expected cold water. But was surprised to be feeling hot water! I would be steaming by the time she cleaned the grit and mud from my belly, paws, and tail. It actually felt quite invigorating to be warmed up while still outside in the cool air!

Once inside, she would dry me thoroughly, shower, while I would lick myself perfect. I was beyond the time of talking back to Olivia, and feeling pretty confident in myself. I was not feeling like a puppy as much, which I didn't know I had been, until I wasn't. The desire to chew and act totally zany for no reason wasn't as strong in me. I knew more, did more, and that made me happy. My Mama would be proud.

As we got settled for bed, I felt a warning tingle in my rough. I stood up, checked the window and gave a little growl, then walked to the deck door and Olivia got the flashlight. We both looked around. I couldn't see anything, but the scent was a raccoon near the edge of the clearing.

After we got re-settled I was just about to slip into sleep, when I saw the soft, blue glow of Brianna. She came towards me with such grace and sat at the edge of the bed in her halo of light. She looked directly into my eyes.

"It is time to claim your full role with Olivia. She has taken care of you like one of her own. She has committed to our ways, she has remembered and followed the Code, and now you must begin to fulfill your greater part. You will fulfill your role as her guardian, using your vigilance and high scenting capabilities to protect her and warn her of dangers."

The timing of Brianna's visit was in alignment with my growing realization that I was strong and capable. The dreamtime had shown me how to utilize my inherent strengths, and drawing on them in the waking life should be no different.

Brianna's glow brightened. I could feel her heart beating, passing her strength and knowledge of the ages to me. Olivia stirred in her sleep. Could she be feeling this ancient energy as well?

Being back at our forest home came with its own set of annoyances I had forgotten while in the land of dry air. The people who lived nearby had two dogs that used their words a lot. They used their words when first let outside, and sadly they used their words while locked in the garage while their people were away.

Getting woken up from naps was one thing, but they also sometimes yammered on at night, which was even more annoying, as I was never sure if their alarming was real or just attention getting. So I would have to get up, and look out the window, or ask Olivia to let me out onto the deck to fully assess. I learned it was shear boredom, imitating a proper announce.

One morning, after too many rounds of this early morning 'wake up the neighborhood with unnecessary words,' Olivia got dressed in a hurry. Her energy was angry, but I was excited by her sense of purpose as we both walked over to the source of the annoyance. Something was finally going to happen!

She was met at the door by a surly older man, holding a mug of coffee. Because I didn't understand most words humans said, I relied on feeling their energy, and how they acted. And their actions told me all I needed to know. As he and Olivia exchanged their own words, his energy was reluctant and she was only getting more frustrated. It all ended with Olivia saying the same words over and over, and the man finally shaking his head, and softening his tone.

In the end I realized, this man was just fine having his dogs yammer at all hours and just fine locking them up alone in the garage for days at a time when he was away. My sense was that Olivia knew this, but she could take no action to change it. She could only use her words. But after the meeting, the dogs announced less often.

A few afternoons later, on one of our walks from home, we came across Shelly, the dog in the cage. I was amazed at how much she had changed. Even out of cage she barely made eye contact with us and kept her distance. Her submissive attitude told me that her life had been very hard since I'd last seen her. The cage had damaged her spirit. It was as if she was still in the cage, even though she was out of it. Sure, she was still friendly and very gentle, but was now a dog spirit who wandered around without a place to fully find comfort.

One sunny morning I heard Olivia on the phone that we were going for a 'hike.' Hike meant we would be going on a trail in the forest with some people! And sure enough, some friends of Olivia's soon arrived at the house.

We all loaded up into one car and Zuma was waiting inside! She was an older dog who looked a lot like my Mama but with different color patterns. She was always kind to me and on the trails kept a slower pace to be by her person. I was usually the zany one on these hikes, but Zuma showed me a way to be more proud and focused. I took note, and after a while stayed with her to be her company.

We had done this hike before, but today we went further on the path than we ever had. The smells, the textures, the forest air and the energy of all of us moving through the forest fully engaged my senses. It was lovely.

Walking with humans through the forest was an ancient ritual that fed deep places in my soul. I knew it fed Olivia's soul as well. As we walked, we walked as one, in the manner of a pack, each of us taking in information, assessing for both dangers and opportunities, peace and connectedness with the life around us. We moved together as we have moved for thousands, if not hundreds of thousands of years, and this day was no different.

The hike left my spirits high that evening. My body felt so alive and strong. It was the longest we had been outside together, and I wanted more. Olivia's heart had been getting lighter every day, I felt it would not be much longer before the clouds would at last lift and we would be fully happy.

She had to heal from many things—some I had seen in flashes as we connected, and of course there'd been the empty house—but I knew each hike and joyous run together was a part of her healing.

As sleep pulled me under, and the comfort of the bed eased my happy but tired muscles, I was again in the vivid dreamtime, but this time I was with Rajyna's clan. Rajyna was right next to me; I was seeing through Kiala's eyes. We were walking together, tracking in the forest. It was dawn. We were moving as one through the quiet landscape. The bond had become strong between us, the glow solid, our comfort and ease we had together was real. That sense of ease and peacefulness remained with me as I woke.

After some breakfast for me and tea for Olivia, we went out for our morning walk. It was early. A hazy, light, serene fog hung in and over the trees. It was not so thick as to block the sun, but rather heighten its strength; everything was brighter. This day was the day of quiet, and I heard very few cars in the distance. The trail was completely empty of dogs and their human companions. There wasn't any fresh pee scent; we must have been the first hikers out that morning.

We passed the splashing waterfall and Olivia paused, saying soft words, and I felt her energy go to the water, and the water's energy go to her. I stopped too, appreciating the joyous rush, as if it were flowing right through me. I jumped down into the rocky grotto to get a few laps of the fresh, cool, bubbling water, then jumped like a deer back up the rocky slope.

Olivia squatted down to pet me and held me close as we both watched the water flow across the jagged rocks, pooling and streaming, and pooling and streaming again. The rush was not the fastest I had seen it, but it had strength enough to push the cool, misty air our way. The scent and sound of the water pulled me back into dreamtime memories; of being in the grassy Highland hills with water plunging from jagged cliffs, of lapping up crystal-clear water from swirling pools. We lingered for a few minutes, enchanted by the sounds, absorbing the ion-charged energy, then resumed our mellow walk, heading towards home.

We passed a section of trail where thick ferns grew high on a bank. I heard a sudden thrashing, and two large dogs shot through the tall green leaves. The first was a long-haired black and brown, wolf-like mix, the second had a red hue to its fur. They were aggressive. They smelled of attack.

The first one lunged for Olivia, I sprang to intercept it. Midair, I glimpsed the red one to my side; he had fanned out to get behind me. I stopped the first dog from tackling Olivia, but the wolf mix was heavier than me; I couldn't hold her off with my front legs, and her jaws sunk into my neck. We were both on our hind legs now, as I tried to keep those jaws from closing around my throat.

"No, no, no, no, no!" Olivia yelled sternly, but this dog was not stopping what it started. Pain seared through me as her teeth drove into my skin; blood began to flow. The scream that erupted from me had undeniable meaning: I was fighting for my life, and I was losing. Then the second dog bit into my rear leg, and my leg threatened to buckle. He kept at me, delivering small bites to my legs to bring me down. I couldn't keep them both away and felt my body slacken from the pain.

My primal scream burst Olivia's protective adrenal scent. She responded with primal force as she lunged for the dog on my neck, yanking it hard enough to break it free from me. She swung the massive beast across the trail with one arm as its jaws gnashed at her face and head, a hair's breadth from her throat. As she turned her head away to avoid a sure bite, she screamed out in pain. But she had transformed; she was fearless; she was now an animal.

As the beast flew backwards hard into the bushes, the other dog was still nipping at me. One knee felt weak, and my other leg was throbbing from the bites. I could now spar with my mouth, but it was too late; my knee gave out. Olivia yelled again, and was fast on the red dog. She kicked it off with enough force to crack bones. And in one swift move, she swept me into her arms, yelling at the dogs as she backed us down the trail.

They turned back towards us. The brown and black one launched again. This time, Olivia was ready, and swung around kicking it hard on the side of the head. A small yelp escaped its muzzle as it dropped to the ground, stunned. Olivia moved in, as if to kick it again, but she stopped mid-strike. She must have felt its determination wavering. The creature stayed down.

Finally, a gruff, portly grey-haired man emerged from

the bushes, calling for his dogs. He had missed the entire attack. Olivia kept backing away down the trail. She was shaking, and I was shaking in her arms. While she held me, she yelled a series of explosive words towards the man. He must have heard the cries of the attack, but had not seen any of it and of course hadn't been there to control or stop his dogs. He had very little to say, and none of it was apologetic or caring.

As he leashed his dogs, Olivia set me down and kept yelling at him, her heart still racing and beating so loudly, I could hear it.

I sensed the man's energy; he felt no remorse, which incensed Olivia all the more. Pointing at my bleeding neck, and my shaking legs, she laid into him again with all her verbal might. He stood, offering nothing, almost proud they had attacked us. She said more angry words to him, picked me up and headed back to the car. On the walk back, she began to cry.

By the time we made it back to the car, I was numb. Olivia was still shaking but strangely calm. Once she lifted me in, she got on her phone. We drove back home. The car was a mess, her shirt was a mess. I was a mess. This was all a mess. Blood was everywhere in weird patterns.

Fresh tears welled up in her eyes when I got out of the car and limped toward the house. Reality was setting in. She was crushed, as if the air had just been sucked out of her lungs and her heart contemplated its next beat. I knew that feeling; it was the feeling I'd had when the car pulled away, leaving brother and me stranded on the road.

She carried me upstairs, something she had not done since I was a puppy, and set me gently on my bed. She grabbed ice wrapped in a towel from the drawer and placed it around my limping knee. She was efficient, but once I was settled, she sat next to me and began to cry again in earnest.

She spoke on the phone briefly again, then started taking pictures of my neck and leg. I was lying on the bitten leg, so she had me stand up and took pictures of the bloody wounds as fast as she could before she let me lie down again. She called on the phone again, and talked with someone, then sat back down next me, petting my head. I wanted to lean up and kiss her, but I was hurting too much, so I stayed where I was, lightly panting, and she leaned over and kissed me instead.

There was a light knock on the door, but I was too out of it to announce. I sensed it was Kaye. The cool towel on my leg was soothing. The piercing pain in my knee had softened to a dull ache, but my breathing had quickened as the pain from my various wounds set in. Kaye came upstairs, and looked over to me. Her energy was as soft and loving as I had ever felt it.

They both sat down next to me, saying kind, soothing words. Kaye brought Olivia a drink from the fridge. She sipped it softly, her eyes distressed. The arm she had used to fend off the dog hung slack at her side. She used her good arm to dab at my wounds with a cool liquid. When I began to pant rapidly, Kaye left but then came back with something for me to eat covered in yummy oil. Whatever it was took some pain away, and I was grateful. Olivia set the cool pack aside and continued to sit by me.

My mind flashed through why I had not smelled the dogs coming. I went through it over and over in my head. What was the wind direction? Oh, it wasn't windy, it was calm. And they came from below us, without a breeze behind them. Nothing to carry the scent to me. It all happened so fast. It was so sudden. I didn't have a moment to give Olivia a warning. I wanted Brianna. I began to pant at these thoughts, and Olivia laid down next to me, petting my back, soothing my worry away. There was nothing I could have done, nothing I could have done. I started to feel sleepy and began to doze.

Sometime later, I needed to go pee. I shifted to get up and felt a zing in my leg. Olivia had dozed next to me on the floor. I didn't know what to do. She stirred but figured it out. She wrapped her arms around my legs, by grabbing the limp arm with the good one, she was able to wrap her arms around me to carry me down the stairs. After the potty, she reversed the process, gave me another coconut oil–wrapped 'yummy' as she called it, and she took one also.

As we settled me on her bed upstairs, her hand on my side, I felt closer to her than ever before. I felt a love for me in her eyes that flooded into my heart. We had survived the attack. She had risked her life to save me, and I had risked mine to save hers. There was no question; given the same choice, we would both do it again.

Kaye came back a few minutes later with her car and helped us get loaded into the backseat. A blanket was laid out, so I could get as comfortable as possible. Olivia sat in the back with me. Even though she was focused on keeping me comfortable, I sensed her arm was in pain by the way she was wincing. Kaye's chatting, kept me a little distracted, but only a little. After a few turns along the familiar busy road, I realized we were going to a place I had been before. The place that had many dog smells.

Once we arrived, Kaye helped us get out. We hobbled in as best we could to the front area and were greeted by a woman who took us back right away. I sensed compassion from everyone in as we limped by. Once I started walking, blood started dripping again, leaving a trail of drops that led to the room. Olivia was doing her best to hold back the wave of emotion I felt rising in her. Kaye was talking with other people; our entrance had sparked several gasps and questions. I'm sure we must have been a sight, my blood all over Olivia, me barely able to walk in.

Both back legs were having issues. The bitten one although painful, was easier to put weight on, but I could barely put my toe down on the other side. That one had me worried, as it didn't feel right at all.

We settled into the room, and they brought in a blanket for me to lie on. A young woman came in with a shallow bucket holding all kinds of wrapped things. She began unwrapping and setting them all up. Then a woman who seemed to be the pack leader, came in and began looking me over while talking with Olivia. Kaye stood by, adding words and feelings to the conversation. The woman was calm and gentle with me, as her fingers carefully probed my body from head to toe. She had a kind manner about her, and was clear in her intention; she was looking into all of my wounds.

I flashed to Jade. All of the scars I had seen on her, this was how they had been made. The woman was feeling my neck; it was tender as she found all the holes and said something to the other woman who was intently watching. She worked her way back to my bloody leg, again giving words to the woman with the bottles and wrapped items.

She began moving the other leg in ways that made it hurt, but she was brief about it. I watched Olivia's face and eyes; it was not good news.

As the younger woman gently cleaned my wounds, the pack leader began to talk with Olivia, pointing at my knee. I sensed whatever she was saying was upsetting. Kaye's face was also unsure. Olivia's energy shifted from open and sad to protective of me. At one point she even became a little angry with the woman. I knew she was fragile from the attack, but as I looked at Kaye's face, there was confirmation of Olivia's protective attitude.

As I limped out of the room, people were all sad around me. I was glad I didn't know what I looked like, and tried to hurry, since a quick hobble put less weight on my weakest leg. She helped me into the car as best she could. I laid my self down in the backseat gingerly, my head on Olivia's lap. She lovingly stroked my head and as we drove away she began to cry.

Exhaustion had pulled me into an uncomfortable sleep, but it was sharp pain and bad dreams that pulled me out. Each bite was repeating itself on my rear leg, over and over, while the jaws around my throat kept pushing in deeper. Olivia was screaming; the dogs' eyes bore into me. I would wake, and it was painful to swallow or move. Blood was still draining from my wounds; its scent on my fur was disturbing.

Olivia could not lie down as she usually did and was sleeping propped against many pillows. She reached out with her good arm to soothe me during my waking cries. As soon as I would slip into sleep, she would cry out. As soon as she fell asleep, I would cry out. The night wore on like this until dawn.

As the morning light came in the window, she looked over my bitten leg and neck. My wounds were still oozing, which made her cry softly. She checked her phone and said the word 'go.' She was talking about going somewhere? Going somewhere today? I was sore and exhausted, sad and in disbelief all at once. I was not even sure I could 'go' to my other bed by her desk.

Today was starting very differently than any other day in my life. I was used to days that started with kisses and pets, playing with a toy, prancing around, happy the morning was here. But now my body was in pain and my soul was weary.

As Olivia helped me off the bed, I hobbled out of the room, finding new painful spots with each step. I quickly laid down on the nearest bed. Olivia brought her clothes upstairs and got dressed in the main room to be near me. I watched her struggle to get her clothes on with only one arm.

After she fed me, she made the arm wrap again to get me down the stairs. Once outside, walking to potty was a challenge, as my body was making each pain more known to me. Although painful to move, I chose to put more weight on the bitten leg, as it was more capable. The other leg felt unstable and was resistant to my weight. So I hopped as best I could for the potty, and then Olivia placed me awkwardly in the backseat of the car as best she could.

We headed in the direction of the beach but kept going. Olivia was on the phone yet again. She was a little teary, and her mood, although tired and sad, had a faint air of hope in it.

We eventually pulled up to a large building and I instantly smelled dogs and cats and horses and many other kinds of animals. The scents distracted me from my pain for a few moments, as I happily followed one over to a patch of grass and promptly peed.

As we hobbled in through the doors, the air had no scent, and the place was clean and bright. Two nice women from behind a tall desk leaned over to greet me, saw my wounds and were sad. This made me sad, but their kind faces were comforting.

They had me stand on a shiny platform for a few moments, after which several rounds of 'good girl' were said to me. Then we went into a very clean, scent free room. The woman asked Olivia many questions, and was patient and kind. Olivia kept petting me, and the woman looked down at me with kind eyes.

Soon a tall man came in. He had bright green eyes and

kind heart energy about him. I liked him instantly, and told him so by greeting him with a wagging tail. He calmly checked all over my neck and back legs. He was very gentle, and his hands seemed to understand where I hurt and why. Olivia's energy softened. She did not feel the need to protect me here, and so I relaxed too. The tall man moved my weakened leg a certain way and gave a soft frown. He didn't like what he felt. Olivia asked him a question, he responded with a nod. She began to cry softly, and said soothing words to me. I knew it had to do with my leg, and since it didn't feel right, it made sense. They were realizing what I felt; something wasn't right with my leg.

They spoke together at length. I was amazed at how comfortable I felt with this man I'd just met. He was kind, but knowing. I sensed he wanted to help me in a way that Olivia was okay with. After more discussion, he got up and the short woman from before cleaned my wounds thoroughly and put cream on each one. The cream was instantly soothing, and she handed the jar to Olivia to put it in her bag.

The woman then pressed into a part of my front leg with something shiny that buzzed. After she was done, my fur was gone from there. That was a very strange feeling; no fur. I looked to Olivia. She was encouraging yet sad. The woman stuck a long, pointed thing into my front leg. It stung at first, but then was okay. Red fluid began filling a tube attached to the pointed thing. After a few moments, she gently pulled it out. That wasn't so bad.

Back home, it was more yummies covered in coconut oil and a nap. Around dinnertime we went out to potty, but I didn't get any dinner. I wasn't too upset, since I wasn't that hungry. Eventually we got settled on the bed as best we could and tried to get some sleep. But just like the night before, neither of us got any comfortable sleep. Dawn came again, and we were both more exhausted, but Olivia wanted to get up anyway. We were going somewhere without breakfast first.

She had an unsettled feeling about her, which of course, made me nervous. After we passed the beach, I realized we might be going back to the place with the nice people and the special cream. Once we turned onto the street that led to the building, I let out a little song of excitement. Olivia's face lit up.

"Amazing," she said.

We unloaded, pottied, and they showed us into a room

right away. Olivia was keeping me close, and gently petting me. She was scared and uncertain about something, but
kept reassuring me, while at the same time not wanting to
leave me. It was an odd combination of feelings for her to be
having. It was if I was going somewhere without her. The
nice man came in again and got down on the floor with us.
I could feel his energy go out to calm both of us. He then
got up and put a different leash on me. Olivia hugged me
close. Wait a minute. She was saying good-bye?

Her energy was calm. She was being strong as she looked
into my eyes. Her message was clear: she would see me later
and I should trust this man. He waited patiently, and understood what was happening. There was a pact between
them, about me. He was to take care of me. And so I went
willingly. I looked back at Olivia, as the door closed behind
me. She was smiling and hopeful and sending so much love.
I trusted her.

The wolf had been with the human family for several moons, and her pups were now fully engaged with the children, looking to them as their siblings.

Most of her time was spent with the hunter on the hunt. She was keen to find scents he would sometimes miss, and would look at him with the intention of sharing. Eventually he began to understand and trust her. His face lit up in wonder at her accuracy and she was instantly rewarded with meat, and a generous warmth from his heart to hers. But she was not yet keen on letting him touch her fur, and he must have sensed her thoughts, as he never moved in a sudden way around her. Their bond of trust was growing slowly.

On the walk back through a shallow snow, she caught a scent that made her hair bristle. Bear. With the dusk closing in, she was even more edgy to get back to her pups. Bear were unpredictable, and with the season changing so erratically, they too may be searching for what was left to forage. She looked back to the man. The scent wasn't strong but he did sense the air, and looked at her eyes. He understood. Within a second the bear was in sight coming straight for them.

They readied themselves, the wolf was nervous. She wasn't sure how to be. A bear would never consider charging a pack of wolves, but she was no longer with her pack. She angled out away from the hunter. He noticed her stance, she was standing with him. Seconds passed she made the first leap, a solid grab on the bear's neck. The hunter was not a second behind, his spear thrusting deep into the bear's chest, the bear raked its claw tearing off the wolf. She was hit hard. The hunter was already close in with an obsidian dagger and thrust it deep into the throat of the bear, as he pulled it out; blood spurted everywhere. The wolf had landed abruptly against a tree, the crack of ribs followed; the bear's life was draining into the snow.

The hunter rushed to the wolf. She was pulling to get up but was stopped by pain, the source was two ribs through her fur. The mans heart leapt with concern as he pulled moss from his bag to stop the bleeding. He looked to her eyes to convey the help, but she already knew he was helping. With the moss applied she struggled to get up and did, but wasn't fully able to take a stride.

The hunter was quick to cut two young trees and fashion his bedding pelt across them. He laid down on it, motioning for her to come to him and do the same. As the bear's groans were softening, she realized he wanted her more than the food. The hunter got up and she laid down in his place. He grabbed one end of the make-shift carrier and began to pull. Across the snow, the ride was fairly smooth, although she never would have been able to walk it in her state.

Once back at the camp, the woman greeted them with surprise. As she saw the state of wolf, she gasped, but made ready for them *both. The pups and the children gathered around as the wolf was laid next to the fire. The hunter shared words with his woman and a burst of love energy surrounded them all. The conveyance of how the wolf saved her man was clear, and now it was up to the woman to save the wolf.*

We walked into a bright, clean, open room full of animals and people. The energy was caring, focused. Metal tables, with walls filled with bottles, and boxes and towels, and other objects I could not describe told me this was a place where a lot was going on. Many people were attending to animals on those tables, and in those cages. Cages? But the people were caring, so this wasn't the scary place old Ted had talked about.

Even though it felt busy, it was calm. Everyone was smiling at me as they brought me back. I was welcome here. We eventually made it to a room separated from the rest of the area; it had windows on all sides. The kind man gently lifted me onto a table, and two woman touched the furless patch on my leg, then stuck one of the pointed things in me. It stung at first, like the last time, but I soon began to drift off. Falling asleep to the sound of their kind voices and assuring touch.

My next memory was of pain and flashes of furless skin; my leg; my belly. Then it was dark. Then pain again, but less so. Then the room was bright. Several people were around me, all wearing colored gowns. The kind man was focused on my leg. Soothing tones were playing. The kind woman—the one who'd taken my fur—was gently petting my head. Where was Olivia, I wondered, as the woman petting me faded to Brianna.

"You're here...why can't I move?"

"They have put you in a great sleep."

I saw my leg was cut open, exposed, raw. They were using something to tie it all together. At the sight of my own blood and tendon, a reflexive jerk moved my body.

"You must stay still and let them work," Brianna instructed.

Then Mama kept licking my head. It felt so good . . . the woman was petting my head. She was smiling. She held something flat and round against my chest.

When I woke again, my leg felt cold to the bone; it was so cold and even more furless. This was not my leg. I began to panic. Something was very wrong. I lurched to get up, but I was dizzy. I couldn't believe it. What had they done to my leg?

I had to pee, but couldn't move, nor could I hold my pee any longer, and so the warm pee trickled out and pooled under me. As I felt the pee start to cool, I didn't know why Olivia had let this happen to me. Why had she let them hurt me this way?

The kind woman, with the help of another woman, gently picked me up, and set me down to clean me. I hopped on three legs, not knowing what to do with the achy, bruised, fully furless thing that wasn't a part of me anymore. I began to shake uncontrollably. Where was Olivia? What if she'd left me? I whined with each breath. What if no one would want me? Now that I was a non-walking dog, scared of myself.

As I was coming back from the cleaning-off area, a door had opened to the main area. And on the other side was Olivia. It was Olivia! I rushed over, hopping as fast as I could, and practically pushed her over. I licked and licked and licked her face over and over and over! She had tears in her eyes at the sight of my leg, but her tears also said it was okay; she was beyond happy to see me.

"You are here! You didn't leave me!" I squealed with delight

She hugged me and kissed me and spoke to me in the way I had grown used to. Then she held me close, and I heard, in the same way Brianna's words would go into me: "Schatzi, I will never leave you." But it was not Brianna's voice. It was Olivia's voice, going straight to my heart. I felt her words. It was truth to me. In a flash, I saw us running together, being happy again. These were her wishes for me. This was our life to be. Even though we were starting from a place where I could barely walk and had an ugly leg, she held this vision for me, for us, and so against all my fears, I began in that moment to believe with her.

We all went back to the cage, and I settled back in. I wasn't sure why I had to go back. I wanted to go home with Olivia. But she reassured me they needed to spend more time with me here. And in truth, as I settled, it felt relieving to be lying down. They hooked up something clear to my front leg, and I quickly began to feel less pain. Oh, yeah, this was feeling way better.

Olivia tucked me into a cozy comforter, and I was feeling a lot safer. I was floating, groggy. It was wrong to be shorn; I started licking the area. A woman came over and covered the leg with a blanket so I couldn't lick it anymore. I shifted to sit up, but it was too difficult, so I just laid over to one side. Olivia was sitting on a chair, holding my paw with her good hand, looking at me with love.

The kind man came into the room. He was smiling, always a good sign with humans. He pulled the blanket back and looked intently at my leg. Olivia seemed relieved at his affirming look. He then cozied the blankets around me. Soon I was fast asleep. I'm not sure how long I was out, but when I woke, Olivia was still there, holding my paw and smelling like chicken. Like the special chicken from the plastic box. Sure enough, she had warm chicken in tow!

My tummy was beyond empty! She was happy to see me awake and excited about chicken. She gave me a few tasty bites. It had never tasted so good! The women were laughing at how focused I was on each upcoming bite. After some more bites, she offered me some water, which I drank and then resettled myself as best I could. There still wasn't any fur on my leg, but the pain was dull at the moment, and I drifted in and out of sleep.

Through my dozing sleep, I heard Olivia asking about the occupants of the cages around me. Directly above me was a Chihuahua who broke his leg when a recliner chair closed on him. Adjacent to him was a Jack Russell boy, whose mama accidentally ran over him in her car while picking up the mail. His mother was beside herself, and had been in few times. Next was a lovely black cat who ate a bird, the whole bird, feathers and all, and had to have her stomach pumped. Right next to me was a pit bull, with his tongue hanging out, who'd hurt his leg also. All of us were hanging out, groggy in our cages, but being cared for. Good people were helping us heal and loving us while they did so.

Olivia spent the rest of the day with me, sitting by my cage, alternating between petting me and holding my paw with her good arm. She fed me chicken every few hours, and watched over me until they asked her to leave. I knew she didn't want to leave me. I didn't want her to leave either, but when I fell asleep, my dreams were peaceful. Soon Brianna was lying next to me in the heather, both of us taking in the sweet smells of the Highlands, a soft sun warming our backs, the fresh air filling our spirits.

When I came back from the dreamtime, the cage room was dim and quiet, but it was definitely morning. I hardly had time to wonder where Olivia was, when she came walking in, beaming at me. The kind man was soon with her too; he was very happy. I guess I was doing well, because I heard the word 'home.' That was just what I wanted to hear! These people were nice and everything, but I wanted to get cozy in my own bed and pee on my own grass.

When we got home, Olivia carried me upstairs, and I saw several more beds for me. One in each room upstairs, and a large gate-type structure surrounded my bed by Olivia's desk. What was with all the beds? And in the bedroom, what looked like a step was positioned alongside the bed I shared with Olivia. I wanted to sniff each of these new items and make sense of them, but I also just wanted to lie down. Olivia set me up on the bed near her desk and I took in as much as I could from that vantage point.

The gate wrapped around this bed reminded me of the cage at the doggie place, but it was much bigger and open at the top. I could see through it to the rest of the house, which made me feel less confined than I really was, and would be right next to Olivia as she worked. My thinking: she wanted me to stay put.

She carried up more bags by herself. That was something new, just watching her do something. I was usually right next to her, helping. That thought gave way to a heavy sigh, and she heard me. "Aww, baby," she said, and came over to kiss my wrong, wounded leg. She knew what I was feeling. Useless.

My leg was now foreign to me and it looked hideous. It was purple, swollen and red and smelled of blood; another sign that something was very wrong. And my belly had a patch of no fur and a fresh cut also. What else had happened while I was asleep?

By way of answering, Olivia laid down behind me, with her arm wrapped around me and one leg really close. She was giving me the body hug. It meant I was still lovable.

Olivia was yawning and completely exhausted, yet she remained highly attentive to me. Checking my wounds, putting cream on them, kissing my bruised and cut leg. She gently cleaned around it, careful not to put too much pressure on it.

In addition to carrying me up and down the stairs with her hurt arm, Olivia had to put me on a short leash to go potty. I went to the grassy area alongside the paved area and kept it quick, as it was very uncomfortable to bend my leg. Back inside, once I got comfortable on my bed, she began talking with me while gently rubbing the muscles of my back and leg. She slowly began moving my leg in a motion that was very similar to walking or running, but done very, very, slowly. I didn't like it, so I pulled my leg away. She gently tried again, so we did a little more, until she sensed I'd had enough. We were starting a new routine.

It was becoming painfully obvious how dependent I was

on Olivia. She was doing everything for me now. Whereas I was in no shape to protect her. Sure, I could sense and hear things and announce, but even that was not as sharp as it used to be. I wouldn't be able to look outside and locate, or get to her quickly if needed. I felt a wave of panic. What was my purpose then? I was not fulfilling my role in the pack! My breathing increased to a soft pant, which I never did while lying down.

Olivia noticed my struggle right away and petted me, saying kind words. Her energy reassured me that I was not alone in my struggle, that she was sad too. But this time I knew she was sad for me. This was a sadness expressed for another, not for herself. I saw in her eyes the journey we were on now. It was a journey to return to the life we'd had. But that didn't happen today. Maybe it would happen tomorrow.

As evening came, Olivia lifted me up on our bed—I was also happy to be in my own bed. No cages, no other people, no other animals around to wake me. The night was quiet, and the lights went out early. Olivia was fast asleep, and so was I, until she woke with a start. She'd had another bad dream. Then I had a bad dream. I felt the dogs rush at me, teeth puncturing my neck. Eventually, we both slept some, but the pain of being on one side was irritating me, and so I started to shift onto the other leg, which took some careful maneuvering on my part. Getting comfortable was difficult, and my rustling woke Olivia, who later went through her own version of trying to get comfortable with her bad arm. We were quite the pair.

The next morning, the routine of the previous day started over. My toe would lightly touch the ground, but I was reluctant to use it, so I hopped on remaining legs, which only made the bitten leg throb with pain. Olivia was scared for me, but trying to be strong and happy. I wasn't sure which part of her to believe.

That night, she set me up on a bed on the floor next to her. I followed her thinking. She hoping we could get some better sleep, while keeping me close. We had a few bad dreams, but all in all both slept a little better.

The next morning I thought maybe I could walk. But with the first touch of the ground I realized I still didn't trust my leg. My bruises were fast fading, and when I was able to lick, I could feel my fur starting to grow back. That was a good sign.

After lunch, Olivia walked me into my crate and zipped me in. She said many kind words, gave me some yummy treats to work on, and she left the house saying, 'good girl.' Of course, I'd been left in my crate many other times, and it wasn't so bad, but that was before, and this time I was scared and hoped she wouldn't be gone for very long.

And she wasn't. She came upstairs calling my name excitedly, carrying a black, plastic case. She unzipped me out of the crate while pointing at the black case. Now I was curious.

She pulled out a small phone-like box and had me lie down. Once she pushed on it a few times, a flickering red light started. She propped the box up on some of my soft toys so it was flickering on the cut on my belly. I was curious what it was doing until it became evident; it was warming my cut in a way that felt strangely good and relaxing. She let it flicker on my belly for a few moments. Then she put the lights that flickered on the cut on my leg, which felt really good. I laid back, sighed and relaxed into it. She was smiling and nodding, happy at the effect. This was definitely helping, and gave us a happy moment.

Our old routine of joy and play was fast becoming a memory. I was now living a new, highly restricted routine, and it made me sad. Olivia had Kaye over briefly, but I got so excited it hurt my leg, I started to limp and had to lie down. Olivia noticed right away, and Kaye did not come over anymore.

It took me a few more mornings to realize I wasn't just going to get up and walk normally again. It was going to take longer than a few days, but I didn't know how long.

Olivia kept doing those strange moves with my leg that I didn't like, but she persisted, and slowly, my resistance to them softened, and she was able to do them to her satisfaction. My favorite parts of the day were when she pulled out the phone thing and let the lights flicker on all my cuts and bruises. That felt great, and so she did it many times a day.

It took many more mornings for me to put my toe down for more than a few moments at a time. It still didn't feel right, but then again, nothing did. This was a new body I had to learn to move with. My bitten leg still didn't feel right to me, and when Olivia looked at my leg, I could see by her face that she didn't think it was right either.

We went again to see the nice man and all the nice people at the place with the doggies, cages and cream. They were all so happy to see me, and I was very happy to see them. I was wagging and putting on quite the show. Olivia did her best to keep me from overdoing it on the slippery wood floor, as I had already done this before, and ended up in more pain. But I was so happy to see some people, that in the moment, I forgot.

Olivia sounded worried when she talked first to a young woman and then to the kind man. His eyes were very thoughtful as he handled my leg. Olivia asked him many questions, and I could sense the stress in her tone. I wanted to go to her, to let her know I would be okay. Even if I didn't know I was okay, I wanted her to think that I would be. But I stayed where I was, as the man continued to check my leg very intently. He nodded and said affirming words to Olivia. But his words said he agreed that something was not quite right with my bitten leg. I knew what they were concerned about. That the bites had done deep damage to my leg.

The moon had cycled, and our once reluctant routine had became our everyday routine. It consisted of being carried up and down the stairs, yummies many times a day, Olivia moving and rubbing down my leg for me, flashing red lights, and keeping me calm. I was losing patience with the passivity. I longed to do things. The things I used to do. And I felt a subtle shift in my mood; my sadness was deepening.

One good thing was my fur had almost grown back; at least I looked like a dog again. I was also lightly touching the ground with my toes when I walked. This gave me some hope. The bitten leg, however, was not moving right, even though I was putting most of my hind weight on it to avoid using the other leg.

Although much time had passed, when I closed my eyes at night, I could still see the dogs coming for me. I would slip into that scary place more often than I would have liked.

I longed for the comfort of Brianna and the dreamtime. I hoped she would come to me; she would help me understand how to run again.

On our next trip to the doggie place, the kind man felt all around my leg and bent it in a certain way. He used a small, thin painful object, like they used after taking my fur. It made the area feel no pain. Olivia was reassuring me petting my head softly. He then used a special painful object, which went far into my leg, and a liquid pushed in. With that, I felt a horrible pain deep in my leg, and was beyond glad it was quickly over. He then did the same thing to the other leg. What was going on here?!

After, I was barely able to stand up, the pain was the worst I'd ever felt and I almost fell over, but Olivia was right there to steady me. She looked horrified until the kind man said words to help her understand. Then she calmed down, petting my back to soothe herself as much as me. I was not sure what had just happened, but I was hoping it wouldn't happen again anytime soon.

Once we were in the car and on the way home, the ache in my legs softened a bit. Olivia gave me many yummies and we went to bed early. I was hopeful that the painful visit would be helpful and slipped into a deep sleep.

It was a dark, gray, cloudy afternoon, a few days after the painful objects visit. The pain had greatly subsided and I was still hobbling around. I was uncertain of how to walk like I used to, but I felt something subtle changing in each of my legs. They both felt tingly, but in a good way, a small stirring of stability. I was happy to have a good feeling in my legs, in any form.

Olivia had been on the phone talking excitedly for a while. As she finished, she gave me a big smile and did a little dance in the main room. Then, she hurriedly started to pack up the big bags. I wasn't sure what all the excitement meant, but packing bags meant going somewhere! Then she started packing things by her desk. That meant we were going to the land of dry air and crickets. Our boring routine was broken! I began to wiggle dance and wag around as best I could. She brought me downstairs and I watched as she started packing her things.

But as I limped over to her to sniff what she was packing, the thought came to me that maybe she would not bring me, because I still was not walking normally. How would that work for me, being down there? So I laid by the bags. I usually did this anyway, but I put extra emphasis on the 'pack me too, Olivia' intention.

She stopped packing and looked at me with such love in her eyes, then hugged me up with kind words. She shared the image of me in the backseat of her car, on my special bed, flying down the busy road with her, peeing in all our spots and licking cream off the top of the cup. Okay, I was coming with her! Of course I was! How silly to think I wasn't. I loved our place down there. It was a lot smaller, which meant I didn't have to go as far to get to my food bowl.

After a few bags were zipped, she loaded me in the car, and we went around town, with Olivia collecting more bags from various places. I had not been in the car for fun since the attack. Just seeing the sites again was making me happy, like part of my former, joyous life with Olivia was making a return. I had a feeling this trip would be good for us both.

The next day she loaded up the car very early in the morning and got me settled in. The backseat was once again set up just for me! She had made it extra soft, and filled it all in with her soft bags, so I couldn't slip into the gap behind the seats. It was also a little higher, so I could see better out the front window while lying down. She had my special car 'harness' on, and clicked me in. She got in the front seat with a big smile on her face, saying kind words to me that had an edge of hope. She had given me extra yummies before she loaded me, and I felt peaceful for the first time since that horrible day. Soon I was dozing, the lull of the road pulling me into sleep.

After some brief images of Olivia carrying me, and taking me potty, I finally found myself in the bright green, sun dappled, dreamtime. I had been longing to get here and was so looking forward to seeing Brianna! I ran with the sheep; my legs were alive and I felt my life as it should be.

I went round and round, remembering the joy of running free over all kinds of terrain, smelling the scents and feeling the breeze. After I had worn myself out, I saw Brianna coming towards me. She was as happy to see me as I her.

"I thought we lost you."

"I have not been able to get back here. It's the attack over and over."

She sighed. A knowing look came over her face. She began to explain; I had been frozen in the moment, unable to move away from it. The intensity of the energy had pulled me into itself, and the only way to not fully fall in, was to look out to the horizon of the present moment, of the moments where I felt love. I sighed with understanding. She was right. The intensity of that day had overshadowed what our life had been, and pulled both Olivia and myself in, for quite some time now. The moments of love were what kept us both going. We were safe now, but we weren't acting that way, not fully. The pain in my legs made the attack ever-present. Olivia's arm was still not the same; I knew her journey was like mine. With that knowledge shared, I felt more peace around how to move forward. I stayed with Brianna most of the day, enjoying the richness of the scenery, whenever I drifted into sleep.

I eventually woke up enough to look around. We had made it past the places of big buildings. Those areas were the most intense, as they usually had the most cars. The road had opened up, and sensing a greater peace in Olivia, I too began to relax.

I felt the car slowing as we went onto a side road. We were stopping in a place we'd stopped the first time we'd done this trip. I actually could smell where I had peed before! I felt joyous at having placed my scent so far from home.

Hour after hour we drove, until the sun started to edge toward the hills. Her explanatory tone conveyed we might be stopping for the day. Soon I could stretch out on a bed and fall into a sleep that wasn't interrupted by the car moving or slowing, Olivia's tones, or singing, or talking on the phone.

We climbed a long hill for a while, then the road went

down, and eventually the car veered to a slower road. We were around buildings again. Olivia was elated when we made it to where we wanted to go for the day. I stood up in the backseat, still favoring my leg. I was more than ready for a leg stretch and a pee-water-food-yummy break.

We were at the place with the mountain with white at the top. I loved the smells, and the crisp air. It had a wild, fresh feel about it. The people were mellow and nice. We stopped at the building we would sleep in, then went on to one of the brightly colored food places. Usually, I would sit with Olivia while she ate outside, but it was too cold out this time. So she left me in the car, ran in, and ran out with a white bag. She hopped in and said words to me while pointing at the amazing food-smelling bag. Read: yummy surprise for me. Back at the sleeping place, Olivia asked me to 'wait' in the car while she carried the bags inside. My leg was starting to ache, but it was better than a few days ago, so I tried not to think about it.

A full day of rest in the car had helped for sure, but it was still not my usual leg. It just didn't feel right, so I tried to hobble faster to get the trip inside over with. Olivia saw this and picked me up with her makeshift arm carry. She carried me inside, up a flight of stairs, and all the way to the room. She set me down outside the door and let us in. I walked a few paces and promptly laid down. She got me water, food and my yummy. I knew I would feel better shortly after. She showered, then laid out a blanket for me upon the bed. I wanted to jump up, out of habit and pride, but she stopped me with a gentle 'no' as I was winding up to make the leap.

Jumping on the bed was part of the fun in coming here, at least it used to be. I was disappointed when Olivia gently lifted me up instead. Even so, it felt good to be laid out, all the way out, with the talking images on, relaxing after a long day. As Olivia ate, she handed me a few pieces of the savory-smelling meat. Enjoying a warm meal at the end of a day lifted my spirits. As we sat together, her breathing softened, and I reflected.

We were staying in the same room we usually did, but we were quite different. My leg wasn't working right, and her arm wasn't either, but here we were together, regardless. So much had changed, and so much had deepened between us. The love, yes, but I felt a little lost in not being able to do what I used to be able to do for Olivia. And that lost feeling left me feeling uncomfortable in who I was. I wanted to return to my former self as soon as possible. It was my purpose, after all! Yet I realized even in my diminished state Olivia loved me just the same, if not more.

We woke to the abrupt sounds of Olivia's phone; the faintest light was coming in through the windows. She was up and focused. She could do that: pop-up out of bed and get going. I, however, liked to wake slowly, and so I watched from the cozy bed, still half-awake, as she quickly packed up and got ready to carry me out to the car.

After I was fed, it was time to potty. Luckily, a wooded area was nearby, and I wandered slowly in the sweet morning air, as Olivia looked after me. I found a good spot well away from anything. I had the urge to run back fast, but Olivia had me on leash for potty now, and held it tightly as she picked up my doodoo. I didn't like being on leash to go potty. I wasn't used to it. And was reluctant to go when Olivia was so close, but here we were, and it felt better to go than not.

Back in the car, Olivia gave me another yummy. My leg was feeling a little better, but it typically did after a good night's sleep. I was thankful for the yummies she gave, and for Olivia's love. She was thinking of how I would feel, how to make me feel better and I was thinking of how she would feel, and how I could make her feel batter. She understood I was in pain, and I understood that she was taking care of me while she was in pain. A very generous offering, an offering only love could provide.

We made our usual stops before getting on the big road: at a window for the cup that had the yummy cream, and then the hose place. After a few turns, we were on the big road, driving really fast. Very few cars were out this early, and I liked it. I sensed Olivia liked it as well. It was easier driving without other cars around. This part of the drive, the car would shift a lot to follow the winding road; which I didn't like. But leaving earlier helped as Olivia could just focus on the road. She had the tones on, not too loud, and we both started to zone out on the road.

My thoughts followed her glances out the window towards the colors and shapes of the distant mountains and trees that flowed out in all directions. It was wild country, and I wished I could run through it all and be free to move, smell, and chase as I wished.

Being back in the land of the dry air was more stimu-lating than being at home, mostly because of the cars. Sure, we lived in a forest of types while we were here, but getting in and out of the canyon, that was the intense part. There were just so many cars, that went so fast. If Olivia was working again, like last time, oh my, we would be in the car a lot! The thought made me a little anxious, but also excited.

We pulled into our place by early evening, and I was so happy to see Hayley and Spot come out to greet us. Big hugs and laughs were exchanged as Hayley helped Olivia take everything from the car and into our home away from home. The paved car path was warm on my feet, and my legs felt instantly better in the dry, warm air. Once inside, Hayley brought down drinks for Olivia and herself, and after some dinner, I was set up with a pizzle. The windows were open, the dry breeze was flowing through and the crickets had started to sing. I could fully relax; we had made it!

Hayley and Olivia chatted late into the evening, then Olivia carried me up to the loft and I let the drone of the car ride fade from my mind and body. Olivia barely moved in the night; she had found a comfortable position and stayed in it. That night my dreams were peaceful, and Olivia did not wake from dreams at all.

Morning came softly into the room. I loved being back up in the loft space. I could look out and feel safe at the same time. Which now, since I was not able to fully protect, gave me a deeper sense of ease and comfort. Today we were sleeping late. Olivia yawned and stretched, and looked with me out to the canyon from our high vantage. She was relaxed, and so was I.

The canyon was very much awake by now. Birds were chirping, the sun was out, and the warmth of the day was flowing through the windows. The nights were cooler here, but the days would warm faster, even during this time of year, the time of low light.

Eventually, I had to pee, and so did Olivia. She went down first, then came back to carry me down, and took me out into the day. It was all familiar to me, and I was excited to take in the scents along the dusty path. As we slowly walked, small lizards scurried out of our way, and birds sang and danced in trees above.

We did our non-work day routine of laying in the sun and napping. Later, we took a drive in the car with the windows down. We went up, past the ridge where we liked to run, and down and over, and onto another winding road. I had never been on this road before. It had lots of hills and bushes and rocks to look at, including some red rocks I had never seen before. The scenery and dry breeze lifted my spirits. We drove in this beauty for a while, until we passed some horses and fences and soon came to a bigger road. A few moments later, we were stopping in front of a set of buildings.

I began to sing. We were going somewhere new! The scents told me this was a doggie place, but as we went inside it was very different. Soft tones were playing, like Olivia would have on in the morning. A water bowl gently burbled, like a stream. Two young women came over to me, and were incredibly sweet. They began talking to me, and petting me, and gave me a soft mat to lie on while we waited. It was like the mat Olivia would go on sometimes and stand in strange poses.

One of the women soon led us into a small room, with soft, gentle lighting and a soft mat. Another woman came in who had a similar energy to the kind man back at the other doggie place. As the woman spoke with Olivia, she put some tiny pointy things on certain areas of my body. They went right into my skin. At first I wasn't sure I wanted all those things sticking into me, but I did feel a welcome lightness come over my body, and it felt relieving in areas.

After she was done, the woman left, and I stayed on the soft mat. Olivia stayed next to me. Soon the woman came back in, out went the pointy things, and she pulled out a flashing lights box. It was just like the one Olivia had! I was excited about that, and it felt soothing all over. She also gave me new yummies.

She then led us to a room at the end of the hall, and we could see a dog walking in a see-through box with water in it. I could see the dog's legs walking under the water, but she wasn't going anywhere. This was the strangest thing I had ever seen! Olivia was very focused on how this dog was moving also. We were both impressed. The walls of the room held rows and rows of colored balls, mats, and toys. The energy was fun and light, both animal and human were having a great time, so joyous. I would be more than happy to come back, and maybe even try that water thing.

The very next day, we were up early. Olivia's small bag went out to the car first, then her chair. Then she loaded my bed, food, and water bowl. I understood. Olivia was going to work and I was coming with her! We were going to the place with many people who looked at moving screens all day! This time we drove towards the Valley, and after some gentle weaving through cars, ended up in front of a blue building. I sang my excitement song; we were at a new place, and new places meant new people.

She helped me out of the car and grabbed her bag. Once at the door; a buzz sounded, and Olivia and I walked in. We were warmly greeted. At the end of a hallway was a big, dark room with many desks and screens. Olivia set her bag on one of them as people shook her hand and asked about me. I was wagging, happy, and felt very welcomed here! It was a little darker than I was used to, but the people were nice and the energy was good. This was a fine work place.

Our new daily routine started very early, with tones from Olivia's phone chirping along with the crickets. She would roll out of bed, get dressed in a hurry, grab a carton of liquid from the fridge and stuff it in her bag. I would wait on the bed, watching this process from above, until she called up to me, "oh, princess!" I would hop down, give a stretch, and wait at the top of the loft stairs, looking down at her. She'd climb up, carry me down and make me breakfast.

As I ate, she finished getting ready, then it was outside. While she loaded the car, I would wait, then we'd go down the side road behind the house to potty. While she was waiting for me, she would pause, take a deep breath and soak up the early dawn. The oak scent of the canyon, mixed with surrounding blossoms filled both our senses. She would stand silently, eyes closed and calm. Sometimes the mist and fog would come up from the coast and settle in around our house. The sun rays would stream through creating an ethereal quality to the scene. Fully immersed, we would bring that feeling with us for our day.

Once I finished my potty, Olivia would open the back door of the car, pick me up and put me in. I'd been embarrassed by this at first, but now I knew it was for the best. My leg was still vulnerable, and there was to be no jumping. I had given in to Olivia carrying me when she thought it was necessary.

She would attach her phone and tones would fill the car. We would back up, face forward, and begin the descent from the house to the main road, where the really fast driving would begin, winding around and finally down to the Valley. Many cars lived in the Valley.

She would stop and go at the hanging lights between home and the busy road, then drive on. Olivia was a smooth driver, and once on the big busy road we mainly stayed in the far side. Sometimes we had to shift around abruptly, and my heart would race, but in general we stayed on the side until we would go to the slower road. This was the shortest ride to work we ever had, and for that, I was very thankful. It made Olivia happy too.

Olivia had her same job of sitting in front of a screen all day, and talking to people periodically, while pointing at her screen, or going into another room and watching other people pointing at a bigger screen. Whew. She did this every day. She didn't seem to get bored. But I was bored about a week in, but I was bored a lot lately as our lives had become very small after the attack. What made it okay for me to be so passive was seeing all the people, and they really liked seeing me too.

One thing that was different about this workplace was it was very dark inside, so dark that my black fur blended in too well, to the point of no one being able to see me! So a few days into our 'studio' routine, the pack leader spoke with Olivia. They were laughing, and he was patting me and she nodded. Then he gently took off my harness and taped a tiny red light and then a green light on me. People could now track me in the dark! Everyone in the studio laughed when they saw me, but at least they saw me.

People would come over and pet me throughout the day. I knew petting me somehow made them feel better, as their energy would change when around me. I might not have been herding sheep, or even Olivia these days, but I was giving the people here something they liked. I was helping in a way that I could.

Eventually our studio day would end, but our day had not ended. Once loaded up, we would get back on the very busy road; it was full of cars and dark outside. Olivia would do her best to breathe evenly and not say mean things to the other cars. We would drive past where we usually turned to go home and instead go all the way to the doggie place. They were always happy to see me.

"Hi, Schatzi!" They would say, and I would wag and sing to say hi back.

This time, instead of little pointy things and the flashing red lights, they took me all the way to the back room and had me walk up into the box that would have the water in it—only no water was in it yet! Olivia was encouraging me all was okay. As I stepped in they slowly closed the clear door behind me. Olivia kept cheering me on and reaching in to pet me. Her eyes told me all was good. Soon I felt a vibration below me, and warm water started filling the tank at my feet. It was like a getting a bath. As the water got higher, I felt lighter on my feet, and a little nervous about what was going to happen, but the encouragement from everyone was very reassuring. Then the pad I was standing on started to move. It pulled me towards the back of the tank.

I stood until my tail touched the back, so I started walking forward to keep from bumping into it. A round of "yay, Schatzi!" went around the room. I guess this was what I was supposed to do: walk on water.

Walking in general had still been painful, but walking in the water was less so because my toes were just lightly touching. In fact, I was floating a little bit. So I kept going, and going, and then the pad stopped moving. After a little rest, we went again. Walking in the water was more work than I thought. I felt like I'd had my first real walk in many moons. It was exhilarating!

After several days of going to the studio, we would have a few days to be at home. Those days were very relaxed and spent laying in the sun. We didn't get up early, we both laid around, Olivia got her clothes clean, and we'd see Hayley and Spot.

But we still went to the doggie place, so I could work my leg. "Oyster Dome," Olivia would say each time we headed inside. I didn't know what that word meant, I just knew I wanted to go hiking with her again. After water-walking, it was the little pointy things and lights—a full day for me. I would limp out, a little tired, but feeling stronger. Afterward we'd stop at a food place, get some yummy-smelling food, then drive the long way home, by the red rocks and horses. With the windows down and my head out the window, I felt free and alive. I would imagine chasing down a rabbit, or sitting atop on of the rocky outcrops, enjoying the mesquite scented vista. The warm, dry canyon air would dry my fur by the time we got home.

After my lunch, Olivia would settle me on my bed with a pizzle, and she would go out to the deck and eat her food with Hayley. These days were easy as we didn't have to deal with all the cars, or sitting and having to wait for Olivia to be able to go home. We were home!

When I was alone, my thoughts could drift without distraction. I dreamt of being able to walk normally, to run and play as I used to. As much effort as we were putting into my leg, it still didn't feel right. It was getting better, yes, but I really thought I would be running by now. I was trying not to be sad about it, but I was sad, as not being able to walk right was becoming my reality.

I knew everyone was doing their best to help me, and for that, I was thankful. I knew I would not end up abandoned, like Ted or Jade. But this wasn't the life I wanted to live, having Olivia take care of everything. Even her arm was still not right, and I knew she was in pain every day also.

So as I heard her laughing on the deck above me with Hayley, with her spirits a little lighter for those moments, I didn't have to worry as much. I just had to rest for now, and dream of running again.

My desire to run was fulfilled, and led me right into the dreamtime. It was sunny, and clear with a strong cold wind. The crispness of the air invigorated my senses.

As I trotted up a rocky rise, I pondered why I was not yet able to run with Olivia. Everyone was helping me and I was strong and healthy, what was I missing? As I watched the soft forms drift across the green below me, I relaxed into the beauty. This was a home I carried with me always.

Amongst the drifting soft forms, a larger directional form emerged from them; it was Brianna. I ran with elation to meet her. As we greeted, she asked me to follow her.

We trotted into a lower valley of the Highlands, and soon were near a fenced area. This was the first time I had been here. We went under the fence up to another rise, where she slowed and sat. In front of us was a site I had never seen. People, with dogs and sheep, and they were involved in some kind of performance. It wasn't a full flock, but enough to herd around, and that was exactly what one dog was doing.

Several other dogs were waiting with their people, and all of them were watching how the sheep were moving to where they needed to go. I was fascinated. I felt my toes grab the soil, my legs twitch in anticipation of how this dog would move those silly sheep. And her human, was right in it with her. Giving calls and tones of direction to his dog. Amazing. It all felt so right, so natural. I wanted to join in.

Once the sheep were in their tiny pen, a round of cheers and clapping erupted. Then, I couldn't believe my eyes, a dog, that looked just like my Mama went out onto the field. The crowd became quiet. I sniffed the air to catch a scent, and looked to Brianna.

"That is your great grandmother."

My eye widened further. I knew it! As she guided the sheep back out of the pen, the tones went to her and she ran them with such grace through all types obstacles and formations. She was more skilled than the dog before her, much more skilled, it was effortless for her. The sheep moved as she 'told' them, and as she finished the crowd erupted again. She remained serious until she slipped under the fence and back into the fold of her elated family. There were two young girls who bent down to kiss and hug her. The glow was as bright as I had seen it. She was magical.

"Do you know why I brought you here?" Brianna asked me.

I didn't know.

"To show you what is possible. To show you what determination looks like." I paused.

"You want to run again, yes?"

"Yes," I replied.

"You have to stay focused. It has to be your main desire. In each moment, find ways to get stronger, that is your job."

Brianna's message was clear. While resting was a big part of my healing regimen, I needed to stay focused on getting my leg better, working to reclaim my agility. This looked like trying to think of my leg first, which I was greatly challenged at, but it gave me a job to do.

Going to work with Olivia helped in that she could keep an eye on me, keep me from jumping and give me all my new yummies as needed. I was able to roam freely at this workplace and greet people as they came in. So it was mellow movement.

It was no secret that I loved to greet people, and they seemed to like it too. Of course, there was another reason why I loved it here: just like at Olivia's other work, they brought in all different types food every few days, and of course Olivia would make sure I got my share.

But the best day of all was when they brought in not just one, but two big chickens! My attention was on the food place that whole day. Once the piles of food had been collected on the counters. They all went outside. It was a warm, sunny day, and they had set up tables in the paved area and set the food out. Everyone filled their plates while chatting and laughing. The energy was big chicken energy; I was not the only one happy to have some. After the great feast, Olivia claimed one of the leftover carcasses for me. She was always thinking ahead.

Our walks around the area had progressed to more than a few minutes at a time, which made us both very happy. I still had a limp, and none of it was comfortable, but at least it was doable. We would do our short walks and hope that the next day I could do more. Olivia would praise my efforts and say the words 'hike' and 'Oyster Dome'. A hike sounded good to me!

After a few moon cycles had passed, less and less people were at Olivia's work each day and we were not staying as late. It had become much less busy. Many hugs and good-byes were shared. Then one morning, Olivia was hugging people, everyone was chatting more, and coming to see me too. She packed everything up, cleared off her desk, rolled out her chair and loaded it all up in the car by the middle of the day. She said some words to me that were a little sad but mixed with relief.

Our drive home had very few cars, which was a first! Once we arrived, she carried me upstairs to the deck, where Hayley had a drink waiting for her.

The feeling was of celebration. Spot and I each got our own frozen bones, and were settled in on our respective

beds, as they sat at the table, overlooking the tree-filled canyon. It was very pleasant to be home with the soft light of
the early evening, as we usually came home in the dark. The
tops of the oak trees changed color as the crickets' cheery
song began.

I relaxed into the moment. My pack was within eye and
earshot; Olivia was safe. I could let my deep senses of vigilance work without effort, the ones I didn't have to think
about. I could drift in and out of sleep – to dream and heal.
Olivia and Hayley laughed into the night and the following
morning, we started to pack. Everything.

Olivia and I were out early into the Valley the next day to get boxes. She packed what she could with her good arm, and the next day people came to take things she couldn't pack. A van was loaded, and most of our things were gone! Olivia was good at packing.

With all the visits to the friendly doggie place and careful walks, I was much improved. I still limped and couldn't jump or walk very far, but my legs were starting to feel more like they used to. I was finally seeing improvement, but it had been many moons now, many moons longer than I had thought it would take.

However, I saw very little improvement in Olivia's arm. It had gotten little attention outside of working and taking care of me. I watched how she held it; she was still in pain, maybe even more than when we had left home. She was strong for me, but even she would need some help.

We went to say good-bye to the loving people at the

doggie place later that day. They gave us both a lot of hugs, and we stayed for a while as Olivia chatted with them all. These were kind humans, and had shown me what was possible. After being with them almost every day, for many, many moons, it would be sad not to see them anymore. They had become a part of my pack. They had helped me in my time of need; cheering me on, wanting me to be healed. They helped me believe that I could be whole again. Maybe I would see them again one day, as a whole, happy dog.

Once back at our forest home, Olivia set up her desk again, and soon after, she was working. We started a new routine, with me walking around the yard a few times a day. I had missed the green grass, and the 'no dust' environment as it was much more humid here.

When I could walk a little further each time, Olivia took me out on the trail near the house or to a local trail where there weren't too many other dogs. Because of the attack, we had to handle meeting other people and their dogs in a whole new way. In general, I just tended to avoid the contact with other dogs unless they had a clear, friendly scent, and very clear tail wagging.

My attitude towards and understanding of other dogs had completely changed since the attack. It had changed Olivia too. She was extremely cautious whenever we met a dog off-leash, let alone one without its owner present. The first dog we'd met on the trail had been off-leash, and I hid behind Olivia when it came racing up to us. Its vibe was not at all friendly. Olivia was now carrying a pole with a pointed tip and used it to keep the dog at bay until his human came to pull him away. She tried to explain the situation and her concerns, but the man was actually mad at her for keeping his dog away.

Other dogs would smell my injury, and if they were in a mood, they'd come after me to prove their strength. It was a dominance move that Olivia had to protect me from. The dogs who came after me had different thoughts and energy scents, experiences of being attacked themselves, people hitting them, their former humans not feeding them, being locked up, or being left alone. In their moments of aggression, they found temporary relief from their pain.

Some dogs approached with understanding; tails wagged, ears remained in open position. There was no desire to control, just a 'hello' and an offer of friendship. Some even wanted to know what happened, or said it had happened to them. I was very happy to meet dogs who were truly friendly, whose owners were gentle, and we dogs would touch noses and sniff and the energy was very calm and fun.

In some ways, I was like Jade, with memories of being attacked, so I was wary. Walking on the trail became a type of game: 'Which direction was the wind blowing?' 'Was a leash involved?' and 'Could we be friends?'

It had been two seasons of the short days and long nights since we were attacked. We had cycled through the inside tree and the big chicken, of napping in the sun and feeling the long light. We had regained more peaceful sleep, and shifted our routine towards how it used to be. I was amazed at how slow, yet fast this time went. The days became very similar, and the changes in me were so subtle, but as we reached the time of the new buds, it was noticeable how far I had come.

I could walk all the way down the trail to where the cars would stay. Even though this had been my original puppy walk distance, I sensed Olivia begin to relax a little more around me as she was happy with my steady progress. We started doing this walk every other day, and although I still had a limp, my stride was getting smoother. My practice in the dreamtime was getting confidence back in both legs! Yet I had no idea it would take this many seasons.

By the following warm season, I was doing a walk every day. Still with a slight limp, but it was more from my leg still being weak than from pain. I had lived with some level of pain since the attack, but now felt less and less every day; my body and spirit were finally coming into balance.

Olivia felt the shift in me, reflecting back my small achievements with a lightening heart. This healing journey had brought us closer in the deepest way possible, as we had to overcome similar obstacles. We became inseparable. The attack bound our hearts together in a way I could only understand in terms of pack: life for life. That fateful day fused our hearts into one, and we had been healing together ever since. My fears of being left or forgotten were long behind me. She was always looking out for me, and I was always looking out for her; we were a pack.

Sadly, her arm had been slower to heal than my leg. I noticed by how she had to use the other one more. She had developed a greater patience with me and herself. She was a different person than when I'd first met her; stronger, more determined, and more compassionate. Our time of healing had changed us for the better, and I wanted nothing more than to share the rest of my life with her.

A few more moons cycled and it was well into the time of new blooms when we did our first short forest hike. The same first hike we did when I was a puppy. I was not as fit as my past self, but I was able to do it. An actual uphill hike! We kept progressing, hiking more and more. Soon I was moving like I used to, feeling no pain. Not long after that hike, we did the same fun hike I had done with Zuma!

The days of long light were here, and the last season had seen me move from a limp to my normal, springy lope, even adding in some periodic leashed running.

When we woke one warm, sunny morning, I sensed an excitement in Olivia; her eyes were bright, and she was humming. She got dressed in hiking clothes and began putting together her hiking bag. I followed her around expectantly, knowing what the preparations meant. It was feeling like we used to feel in the old days: getting ready to go somewhere fun; the trail!

I jumped into the backseat of the car, and we were away with the windows down, my head in the breeze! We were headed towards the beach, but we drove right past it and kept on going until Olivia pulled over to the side of the road. We weren't quite to the open plains and had never stopped here before. I began to sing, "Where were we going?"

Olivia looked back at me with a huge smile and said some words that matched my song. As soon as she put my harness and leash on, I was prancing to get going! This new trail started out right off the road and it was steep. Back and forth we went, up and up and up. My muscles were all working together; my strength and balance had returned.

Through the huge trees along the trail I could see the gray-blue of the water far below us. We were getting higher rather quickly. On we went, passing over soft-running trickle streams and exposed tree roots. The trail fueled me, but I was steady and measured in my pace. I could sense by Olivia's pace this hike would be longer than any we had done yet.

Given it was early morning, we hadn't seen anyone else so far, it was just the forest and the trail. I was focused. My heart was pounding at just the right beat. My legs were moving in perfect stride and lope. It was all just happening; no thinking about it, no forcing, just gliding along the trail. I strode confidently in front of Olivia and took the lead. My role was fulfilled again in the pack.

A series of images began to flow—the pain, the travel, the pointy things, the sadness, the bad dreams, the attack, even the small victories along the way. The corresponding feelings of worry, struggle, the doubts and sleepless nights, their ever-present weight began to shed off me. It all began to fade. Every step forward lessened their presence in me. The fullness of the moment overtook me. My senses filled with the trail. I felt lighter with each step. I was coming home to myself. My own nature flowing through me again.

We reached a point where the trail became really steep, I accessed my deeper strength, and it responded; hopping and navigating the roots and rocks the higher we went. Higher and higher we went, until we reached a large creek, where I savored a quick drink. It tasted ever so good after the climb.

As we passed through the water, its cooling sensation further invigorated my soul. We made it to another rise that flattened out. I sensed Olivia's heart become calm. This section was covered in a blanket of vibrant green moss; gently lit through the trees. It was soft and had an ancient, untouched-by-humans feel. Then the trail veered upward again, with light sky blue through the trees ahead.

A joyous wave grew in me, my fear of never being able to do a hike like this had dissolved. I felt like I did when I was in the dreamtime; full, alive and free. My resolve increased as we continued up the next section; the trail evened out a little and the ground felt springy. A light breeze picked up on the rise. As we neared the edge of the forest, Olivia was at my side. We broke out of the forest and onto a rocky precipice.

"Oyster Dome," Olivia whispered.

My heart soared at the expansive sight of small islands and blue waters spread out below us. It was the largest view I'd ever seen, and the highest I had ever been. We sat quietly, side by side, looking out across the valley, over the rippling waters and distant lands, as the sheer drop let us see far and wide around.

Olivia smiled at me. Her eyes connected with mine, so full of love. We were here. We were whole again. After everything, we'd made it. We were living the Code, and we had the rest of our lives to share days like today.

The familiar tingle grew in me, it was Brianna, it had to be! I looked along the rocky ledge to find her, and as I was scanning to my other side, she settled in next to me; so majestic and calm, taking in the beauty with us. I was unnerved. This was not the dreamtime, this was this time. I wondered if Olivia could see her as I did. I wonder if she felt her?

I looked back towards Olivia, and she was now Rajyna.

"Amazing," she said.

Yes, it was.

the
DREAMTIME

The second book in the Kiala Trilogy, *the Dreamtime*,
takes Olivia deep into Schatzi's world.

...2017 release...

Made in the USA
Columbia, SC
29 November 2018